St. Helens Libraries

Please return / renew this item by the last date shown. Items may be renewed by phone and internet.

Telephone: (01744) 676954 or 677...
Email: libraries@sthe...
Online: sthelens.gov...

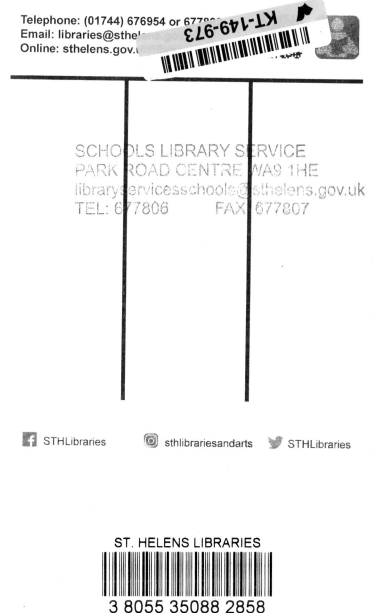

STHLibraries   sthlibrariesandarts   STHLibraries

ST. HELENS LIBRARIES

3 8055 35088 2858

EDDIE ALBERT

AND THE AMAZING ANIMAL GANG

 PAUL O'GRADY

ILLUSTRATED BY SUE HELLARD

HarperCollins *Children's Books*

First published in the United Kingdom by
HarperCollins *Children's Books* in 2021
Published in this edition in 2022
HarperCollins *Children's Books* is a division of HarperCollins*Publishers* Ltd,
1 London Bridge Street
London SE1 9GF

www.harpercollins.co.uk

HarperCollins*Publishers*
1st Floor, Watermarque Building, Ringsend Road
Dublin 4, Ireland

2

ISBN 978–0–00–844683–3

Paul O'Grady and Sue Hellard assert the moral right to be identified
as the author and illustrator of the work respectively.

A CIP catalogue record for this title is available from the British Library.

Typeset in Arno Pro 12pt by Palimpsest Book Production Ltd, Falkirk, Stirlingshire
Printed and bound in the UK using 100% renewable electricity
at CPI Group (UK) Ltd

*Dedicated to everyone both young
and old who talks to their animals*

AUNT BUDGE

EDDIE

BUTCH

DAD

VERA

CASEY

DAN AND JAKE

BUNTY

STANLEY

PROLOGUE

D o you have a secret? Is there anything about you that you'd much rather keep to yourself? Maybe you've done something in the past that you're ashamed of? You might have told a big fat lie, or invented wild stories about yourself and your family, when really you don't live in a mansion or own a pony but actually live in a perfectly ordinary house or flat.

You might have an unusual hobby or interest that you don't talk about in case people who don't understand these things think you're weird. Then, of course, there's that nasty habit you might have that you'd rather no one knew about, like nose-picking, eating belly-button fluff or not wiping your bum. Ugh.

This story is about a young boy called Eddie Albert who had an amazing secret. If you sat next to him on a bus or walked past him in the street you'd be forgiven for thinking

1

he was just an ordinary ten-year-old boy. A bit scruffy, perhaps, not very tall and with an unruly mop of blond hair, but nothing in the least bit remarkable about him.

Well, you'd be wrong, for Eddie Albert possessed a truly extraordinary talent, a unique skill that he really should have been very proud of. Only he wasn't. He was extremely secretive about his hidden talent, determined that nobody should ever find out about this awesome gift that he saw as more of a curse. It had got him into trouble at school several times, and today was one of those days. It all started because of a mouse . . .

CHAPTER ONE

Eddie wasn't really what you'd call naughty. He wasn't a bad kid at all – in fact, he was quite the opposite. But trouble seemed to have a nasty habit of following him around, and it usually involved animals.

Once, Mr Broad, the PE teacher, had gone ballistic when he found Eddie on the school roof. But Eddie hadn't shinned up the drainpipe and on to the flat roof for a dare or to show off. In fact, he'd wanted to rescue a seagull that was trapped between two planks left there by the builders who were repairing the roof.

Nevertheless, Eddie had been hauled off to the headmaster's office and given a long lecture on health and safety and the stupidity of little boys who liked to impress their friends by climbing on roofs.

He'd been late for school on a number of occasions as he was always stopping to help lost or injured animals when he took a short cut through the park. One winter's morning he came across a grass snake that was half frozen from the cold, so he popped it into his rucksack to get warm. Once it was nice and toasty, the snake woke up and decided to go for a little slither around – which of course happened during English class. Eventually, it settled on Miss Pike's foot. The English teacher fainted and once again Eddie found himself standing before the headmaster's desk. The man couldn't understand how it was possible for such a quiet little boy to get into so much trouble.

Eddie loved all animals, and people thought he had a special way with them.

'It's as if he can understand them,' Mr Ali, who ran the local shop, would say. 'My cat likes to sit on the step and Eddie always stops to talk to her on his way to school. Now, my cat is very fussy and doesn't take to strangers, but she loves Eddie.

She meows and purrs and wriggles about and he answers her. Quite a conversation they have! As I said, it's as if he can understand her . . .'

The thing was: Eddie could understand animals.

Highly improbable as it sounds, Eddie Albert could converse with mammals, birds, fish and even snails (although snails do tend to have a limited vocabulary that involves a lot of slurping and hissing) just as well as with humans. It was an incredible gift, but Eddie didn't see it that way. He was the kind of boy who didn't like to draw attention to himself, preferring to get on with his work rather than mess about, which made him a frequent target for bullies.

Eddie was determined to keep his special talent firmly under wraps. He was scared that if it was discovered he'd be seen as an oddity, a freak. He'd be ridiculed by the tabloid newspapers and people would point at him in the street. He'd be all over social media and made to go on daytime television and have to prove his talents weren't just a trick. He'd be world-famous, unable to go anywhere without people wanting selfies and demanding that he speak to their dogs.

No, no, no! That wasn't going to happen. A bit of fun with Mr Ali's cat could be taken for a young boy play-acting, but apart from that he kept his amazing capabilities to himself and only used them when no one was around.

Now, where was I? Oh yes, I was telling you about a mouse, the one that caused all the trouble. It appeared from underneath the radiator in Eddie's classroom during a maths lesson one afternoon and, for something so small, it caused a lot of problems.

CHAPTER TWO

From the way the mouse was just sitting there, staring round the classroom, Eddie could see it was lost. He bent down as if he were looking for something in his bag so he could talk to it.

'Psssst!' he hissed. 'What are you doing here? Go home.'

'You couldn't tell me how to get to the boiler room, could you?' the mouse asked politely, giving his whiskers a quick wipe with his paws. 'I seem to have taken a wrong turn.'

'Why don't you go back the way you came? Only head downwards as the boiler room is in the basement,' Eddie whispered.

Unfortunately, he was overheard.

'Miss!' Quentin Harris, the class snitch and a grade-A bully, shouted out so loudly that the entire class turned round.

Quentin sat at the opposite end of the same table as Eddie and he loved nothing more than to suck up to the teachers by ratting out his classmates.

'Miss!' he shouted again, even louder this time.

'What is it, Quentin?' Miss Taylor asked. She stopped writing on the whiteboard and looked round in irritation.

'Eddie Albert's talking to himself, miss,' Quentin replied, beaming with smarmy self-importance and sheer delight at the thought of getting Eddie into trouble.

'I was not, miss,' a red-faced Eddie protested, sitting up quickly in his chair.

'Then you were talking to the radiator. I heard him, miss,' the smug Quentin whined on, determined not to let the matter drop. 'He told it to go home to the boiler room. He's a nutter, miss. Fancy talking to a radiator!'

The entire class thought this hilarious and started laughing and sniggering until Miss Taylor told them to be quiet and reminded Quentin that the word 'nutter' was offensive.

'Eddie,' Miss Taylor said, leaving her desk and walking over to him, 'you wouldn't have a phone in your bag, would you? Because you know I don't allow phones in my classroom.'

'No, miss,' Quentin assured her. 'He hasn't got a phone because his dad works in a supermarket and can't afford to buy him one. I've got a phone, a tablet and a brand-new computer, miss.'

'Then you're a very lucky boy, aren't you?' Miss Taylor told him with just a hint of sarcasm in her voice. 'When you get home, why don't you look up the words bragging and boasting on this brand-new computer of yours. Now, be quiet.'

Turning to Eddie, she asked him what all this fuss was about. Had he been talking to anyone and, if so, who?

Eddie liked Miss Taylor. He wasn't very good at maths but she was very patient and kind, taking time to explain the really hard things to him. Today he thought she looked tired and, as he didn't want to lie to her, he told the truth.

'I was talking to a mouse,' he said to her calmly.

Eddie might just as well have announced that he'd been talking to a six-metre-long man-eating snake, as the word mouse caused immediate mass panic.

Miss Taylor quickly glanced at the floor, wrapped her skirt round her knees and moved away. If speed-walking backwards, knock-kneed because you're holding your skirt tightly round your legs, had been an Olympic sport, then Miss Taylor would've won the gold medal.

'Calm down, children!' she shouted as pandemonium broke out. A lot of the girls were screaming and climbing on to their chairs, as were a few of the boys. Some of the children were adding to the mayhem as they ran round the classroom, shouting, 'There it is!' and 'I'll catch him!' One of the boys picked up a girl's cardigan from the floor where it had fallen from the back of a chair and gave it a good shake. In doing so, he sent a chunk of chocolate that had been in the pocket flying across the room in the direction of Miss Taylor.

At the sight of this little brown thing coming towards her, Miss Taylor let out a scream that could have shattered glass and leapt on to her desk with the speed of a kangaroo.

Just then Mr Pickard, the headmaster, walked in.

'What's going on here?' he demanded, clapping his hands loudly in an attempt to silence the class.

'There's a mouse!' Miss Taylor gibbered from her perch on top of the furniture. 'It's underneath my desk right now . . . a big brown mouse! Oh, dear me.'

Mr Pickard – known to quite a few of his students as Mr Pick-on because that's what he did to you if your work wasn't up to scratch – bent down slowly and looked under Miss Taylor's desk. The class fell silent as everyone held their breath.

'Is this what you're looking for?' he said, standing up after a while. He held something in his clenched fist.

A girl started screaming again as Mr Pick-on held out his arm, slowly opening his hand. *'Voilà!'* he shouted, like a magician who'd just sawn a lady in half.

Miss Taylor, who'd been just about to let out another bloodcurdling scream, saw that the 'mouse' the headmaster was holding was actually just a piece of chocolate.

'I feel such a fool,' Miss Taylor stammered, blushing a deep red as she climbed down from her desk. 'You see, Eddie Albert saw a mouse over there by the radiator and I went—' But before she could finish her sentence Mr Pick-on stopped her.

'Eddie Albert again,' he sighed, shaking his head slowly. 'I might have known you'd be responsible for this chaos. My office, please. Now.'

Just as I was telling you, trouble seemed to follow poor Eddie around, and it usually involved animals.

CHAPTER THREE

'It's not fair,' Eddie said aloud to no one in particular as he walked home from school. He hadn't had a good day. It had started badly when he got up and discovered an empty fridge with no milk for his breakfast Weetabix because his dad had forgotten to buy any again. He poured water on them instead, which wasn't that nice but, as he told himself, was better than nothing.

His dad had left the house already for an early shift at Wise Prices, the budget supermarket where he worked, but Eddie was used to that and quite capable of getting himself ready for school. Even if it did mean wearing the same shirt for three days on the trot, which he was having to do today as he didn't have any clean ones.

Then he'd had a rotten day at school, culminating in that trip to the headmaster's office for a telling-off for something that wasn't his fault.

'I hate that school,' he said aloud, kicking a bottle top into the gutter. 'I'll be glad when the summer holidays start so I can get away from the whole stinking lot of them.'

'Talking to yourself again, Albert?' Quentin Harris shouted as he came out of the fried-chicken shop, carrying a bucket of wings. 'Or have you got that mouse in your pocket?'

Just ignore him, Eddie thought to himself and carried on walking.

'You're crazy, you are, a loony lunatic. You should be locked up for talking to yourself all the time. Are you listening to me, mouse boy?' Quentin goaded, poking Eddie in the back as he walked closely behind him.

Determined not to give in, Eddie simply pretended that he hadn't heard. He very rarely lost his temper but Quentin was certainly pushing his buttons at the moment.

'Are you deaf as well as daft?' Quentin went on relentlessly, trying to trip Eddie up now. 'You should go to a school for freaks. It's not safe having someone like you around. That's what I think and I'm going to tell everyone to keep away from you because you're dangerous.'

'Whatever,' Eddie muttered as he kept on walking.

'You won't even eat chicken,' Quentin continued, waving a greasy wing about. 'You're weird.'

'Why?' Eddie replied calmly as he carried on walking. 'Because I don't believe in eating animals?'

'A sausage isn't an animal,' Quentin scoffed. 'You're a nutter, that's what you are. I love eating meat – we have it every night for dinner in our house,' he bragged. 'You only eat rabbit food because that's all your dad can afford.'

'Why don't you keep your stupid opinions to yourself?' Eddie snapped. He spun round to face his tormentor. 'You're always creeping around the teachers and telling tales. You're a snitch, and it's no wonder you've got spots all over your face, and your bum is bursting out of your trousers with the amount of junk food you eat,' he added for good measure.

Quentin's face turned scarlet with rage and he started to shake. 'I have not got spots . . . it's a heat rash. And I have not got a big bum!' he spluttered.

'Yes, you have,' Eddie teased. 'There're two things you can see from the moon – the Great Wall of China and your bum.'

'You can't talk to me like that,' Quentin whined. 'You're not allowed to because I'm special,' he said proudly. 'I've got anger issues and get very upset if anyone's nasty to me because I'm sensitive. The school psychologist said so – she told Mum and Dad. So there, mouse boy – stuff that up your jumper.'

Eddie looked him up and down slowly. He was feeling very brave right now and all the anger and pent-up frustration from his rotten day gushed out like air from a burst balloon.

'Call it what you want,' he replied, 'but really you're just a spoilt mummy's boy with a spiteful temper that you can't control. Where is Mumsy today? Isn't she picking you up in the car?' he teased, really going for it now. 'Don't tell me she's letting her lickle baby walk all the way home by himself?'

Quentin looked as if he were about to explode, but, as his rage had temporarily robbed him of the power of speech, all he could manage was a gurgling noise that sounded like an ostrich having a drink.

'And another thing! Stop texting Sandra Ellison – she doesn't fancy you and wouldn't go out with you if you were the last boy on earth. I heard her telling Devorshka,' Eddie went on, oblivious to the steam coming out of Quentin's ears and nostrils, 'that she thinks you're a great big pig-faced—'

But, before Eddie could continue, Quentin completely lost his rag and punched him as hard as he could.

CHAPTER FOUR

'Honestly, Eddie,' his dad said, frowning and tutting as he dabbed antiseptic on Eddie's cut lip. 'First I get a phone call from your headmaster to say you've been disruptive in class and then you come home with blood all down your shirt and a cut lip because you've been fighting. What's the matter with you?'

'I wasn't fighting, Dad,' Eddie protested, wincing as he patted his lip with a bit of kitchen roll. 'Quentin Harris just punched me in the mouth.'

'For no reason?' his dad enquired. 'He just hit you?'

'Well, we were having an argument, you see, but he started it. And then he hit me,' Eddie explained.

'And what did you say to rile him up like that?' his dad asked.

Eddie kept quiet, pretending that his cut lip made it hard to speak.

'Come on, out with it. What did you say?' Dad persisted. 'I know you've got a sharp tongue if somebody gets your back up.'

'I said he had spots and a fat bum,' Eddie replied, smiling as he remembered the expression on Quentin's face.

'Did you now?' his dad said, trying not to laugh in spite of himself. 'That's not very nice, is it?'

'Well, he's not very nice,' Eddie responded. 'He's a bully and he's always telling tales to the teachers and he said you were poor cos I haven't got a phone and he has.'

'Listen to me, son. Boys like Quentin aren't worth wasting oxygen on. Just ignore him, pretend he doesn't exist and don't let him get to you,' his dad advised. 'There's a lot more to life than mobile phones – and they're certainly not worth getting into a fight over. I've told you before: you can have a phone when you go to big school.'

'But I didn't start it,' Eddie almost shouted. 'He hit me!'

'Well, you did give him a right mouthful and, whether he deserved it or not, you know he has problems controlling his temper,' Dad replied. 'A cruel word can be just as hurtful as a punch.'

Eddie folded his arms and sank down sulkily in his chair. He felt like exploding with the injustice of it all. It wasn't fair that his dad considered him to be partly to blame, even though he was the one with the split lip and not Quentin Rotten Harris who'd started it all in the first place.

Typical, he fumed silently. *I always end up getting the blame for everything. I bet if the street fell into a sinkhole it would somehow be my fault. It just isn't fair. It's rotten.*

'I'm going to start a union for kids,' he told his dad, 'and, if a kid's got a complaint against an adult, then they have to go to court where the evidence can be looked at properly before innocent people get blamed for something they didn't do.'

'You do that,' his dad replied absently. 'Now, why don't you go to your room and feed your animals while I rustle up something to eat? And then I've got some important news to talk to you about after tea. I'll let Butch out of the kitchen first; he's been driving me mad with his yapping.'

Butch was a Jackawawa – that's part Chihuahua and part Jack Russell. On his way home from work one night, Eddie's dad had bought him from a man who'd been staggering around outside a pub, waving the tiny puppy in his hand. Eddie's dad was determined to get the poor creature off this sleazy-looking character as it was obvious he was incapable of looking after himself, let alone a dog.

Dad had known that if he was to get the pup away from this bloke he'd have to be extremely crafty.

'Can I have a look at your dog, mate?' he'd asked casually, putting on a cheerful voice. 'What sort is it?'

'Dunno,' the man slurred, leaning against the wall of the pub. 'I've been trying to flog him in there –' he nodded towards the pub door – 'but the landlady chucked me out. Here, have a look at the little rat, if you're interested.'

Eddie's dad had held the tiny pup in the palm of his hand. It was dirty and half starved and one of its eyes had closed over, the eyelid swollen and clearly infected. He was sickened at the state of this pathetic little dog and he desperately wanted to tell the man what he thought of him, but he bit his tongue and played it cool so as not to make him angry.

'Doesn't look like it'll last the night,' he said casually. 'How much do you want for it?'

"Undred quid,' the man replied, belching loudly and putting his hands on his knees to steady himself.

'You won't get a hundred pounds for this,' Eddie's dad said, shaking his head as if he was an expert. 'It's a mongrel, and half dead at that. And besides I haven't got that kind of cash on me.'

'How much you got, then?' the man asked, lurching towards him.

'I've got five quid,' Eddie's dad said, for that was all the money he had on him. 'Take it or leave it. I'll be doing you a favour taking this off your hands.'

The man thought about the offer for a moment before eventually shouting, 'Done! Now, gis the money and you can 'ave it!' He'd snatched the five-pound note out of Eddie's dad's hand and staggered off down the road, leaving him alone on the pavement with the tiny pup shivering in the palm of his hand.

'Come on, little one,' he'd said, putting the puppy inside his coat to keep him warm. 'You cost me my last fiver, which means beans on toast for dinner for Eddie and me. Now, let's get you home.'

Of course, Eddie had fallen in love with the pint-sized puppy the moment he set eyes on him. He was really very sick, though, having been taken away from his mother far too early, but Eddie decided to nurse him back to health.

'What shall we call him, Dad?' Eddie asked as he cleaned the little dog's eye.

'Call him an early birthday present,' Dad said. 'But we've got to keep an eye on the little fella as he's quite poorly.'

The dog really was very sick indeed. But Eddie, who was in tune with all animals, knew what this little pup needed – and that was lots of love and constant care, which Eddie was only too happy to provide by the bucketload.

CHAPTER FIVE

Eddie's bedroom had become a sort of animal hospital over the years. He'd looked after a wide assortment of injured birds and had become quite an expert at mending broken wings. He'd hand-reared baby hedgehogs, a barn owl chick and even a stoat with a broken leg. Once they were well again and able to care for themselves, Eddie released them back into the wild where they belonged. So for the moment he only shared his bedroom with Butch, two goldfish named Dan and Jake, and a hamster called Bunty.

Believing that the news Dad was about to break to him was more than likely going to be bad, Eddie stomped moodily into his bedroom, followed closely by Butch, who was yapping his head off as usual.

To anyone else's ears, Butch's yapping would be just that – an excitable little dog barking incessantly. Nothing in the least bit unusual. However, Eddie heard something else entirely.

'So tell me what happened?' Butch asked Eddie eagerly as he ran round the room. 'Did you let him have it? Eh? Did you run him out of town? I'd have bitten him on the ankle and ripped his trouser leg off,' he continued without pausing for breath. 'How did it start?'

'A mouse came out from behind the radiator in class,' Eddie explained. 'He was lost, you see, and just as I was telling him how to get to the boiler room—'

'Why?' Butch interrupted. 'Was there a party going on in this boiling room or was it the headquarters for the Mouse Mafia and this mouse was a trained assassin?'

'I don't know what was going on in the boiler room,' Eddie replied, laughing. 'But, just as I was telling him how to get there, Quentin Harris heard me and told the teacher. Then afterwards he started on me as I was walking home.'

'The big bully,' Butch growled angrily. 'I'd have keeled him. I'd have hunted him down like a dog.'

'You are a dog,' Eddie reminded him.

'Doesn't matter,' Butch growled. 'I'd still have keeled him.'

When Butch was angry, which he frequently was, the Chihuahua side of him

came out and he spoke in what he considered to be a Mexican accent (as Chihuahuas originated from Mexico). This accent was extremely dodgy because he'd picked it up from watching old cowboy films on daytime television.

Butch loved these films and, after watching one, he'd swagger round the house, speaking through gritted teeth. He'd say things like, 'This town ain't big enough for the both of us,' and, 'I've come for my boy,' in his roughest growl.

Eddie always thought Butch really believed that he was a great big dog – as little dogs so often do – whereas, in fact, he was tiny. Tiny but very, very tough.

Butch also loved the heat – claiming it was down to his Mexican blood – and could normally be found sitting bolt upright with his eyes closed in front of the gas fire, basking in the warmth, or stretched out in the park on the hottest of summer days, taking in some rays as he liked to call it.

Eddie sat on the edge of his bed to take his shoes off, but was disturbed by a loud tapping at the window. Turning round, he was greeted by the sight of a large black bird sitting outside. The bird tapped on the glass again with his beak and shouted, ''Urry up and open the window, will ya? It's starting to rain out 'ere and I'm gettin' soaked.'

'Well, if it isn't the Liver Bird,' Butch said sarcastically. 'What does he want?'

The Liver Bird was a crow. Eddie had found him as a chick when visiting his dad's brother, Uncle Jack, in Liverpool. He'd fallen out of a nest in the local park and, as there was no sign of his mother, Eddie brought the chick home and hand-reared him, knowing instinctively what to do even though he was only eight at the time.

His dad had brought Butch home not long afterwards, so the pair of them, dog and crow, had sort of grown up together. Now they were older, there was a little bit of sibling rivalry going on. The crow's real name was Stanley, because he'd been found in Stanley Park, but Butch had christened him the Liver Bird after the statue that sat on top of the Liver Building overlooking the River Mersey.

Two years after Eddie had first found him, Stanley had grown into a healthy, happy and highly intelligent crow,

and although he no longer lived in Eddie's bedroom, having flown off some time ago, he still made regular visits.

Eddie opened the window and the crow hopped in, landing on Eddie's desk.

'Hiya, Stanners,' Eddie said, stroking the back of the bird's head. 'D'you want a rub-down with a towel? You're a bit damp.'

'No need, the plumage is water-resistant,' Stanley said, giving himself a shake. 'But I'm glad you're here as I was getting drenched sat on that windowsill. By the way, did you know your gutter's leaking?' With that, he shook himself out again, quite violently this time, and started to preen his right wing.

'Gets on me nerves, that feather,' he said, straightening a large black feather that was sticking out at an odd angle. 'Never lies flat no matter what I do to it. You haven't got any gel, have you? Or a hairclip? Maybe I'll leave it and if anyone comments I'll just say it's a fashion statement. Right then,' he continued, changing the subject, as he was frequently inclined to do. 'Maths homework. What is it tonight?'

'I've got to find the percentages of fractions,' Eddie sighed miserably. 'Miss Taylor gave me extra homework.'

'Easy-peasy,' Stanley replied, hopping about on the desk. 'No need to sweat. I'm brilliant at fractions, absolutely brilliant. And I can answer all the questions on *University Challenge* although I don't see it very often as I haven't got a telly. But don't you worry about fractions – I can do them standing on me beak.'

'Well, I can't,' Eddie moaned. 'I haven't got a beak and I certainly haven't got a clue what Miss Taylor is talking about most of the time. Even if she is really patient, it just won't go in. Maths is all mumbo-jumbo to me.'

Stanley reassured him that, with his great knowledge of all things mathematical, by the time he'd finished with Eddie he'd be a genius.

Butch, cocking his head to one side, was very dubious about this. He asked Stanley just how he knew all these things, and was there really any point in learning about fractures?

'I think you mean fractions,' Stanley corrected him. 'A fracture is when you break a bone.'

'Well, whatever they are, they both sound painful,' Butch replied, yawning. 'Painful and boring and I don't see the point of learning 'em.'

'There's always a point to learning,' Stanley replied knowingly. 'Education is knowledge, little bro, and with it you can go far in life – have knowledge, will travel. Or, in my case, it's have wings, will travel!' He flapped his enormous wings and let out a raucous cackle, unnerving Butch and sending him scurrying under the bed, yapping fretfully.

'Couldn't agree with you more, Stanley,' Bunty the hamster said, stepping through the front door of the old doll's house that Eddie's dad had converted into a suitable home for her. 'Flying is simply the best,' she said, stretching out her front legs as she yawned long and hard, revealing a set of very sharp teeth. She was a typical hamster, little and rotund with a golden coat and a white furry belly.

You probably already know this, but hamsters are nocturnal, which means they sleep all day and then are busy all night. But Bunty had managed to turn her body clock round, as she was bored being awake when everyone else was sleeping because it meant she had no one to talk to.

Now, she was awake in the day and went to bed when the others did. On the odd occasion, though, she did like to take a little nap of an afternoon.

'Flying really is a splendid experience,' she declared again once she'd finally finished yawning. 'There's nothing to compare with the thrill of taking to the skies. Why, I remember flying across the Channel frequently with

30

Roger.' She paused to explain to Stanley for the hundredth time who this Roger was. 'He was a pilot in the RAF, you know,' she said, standing with her legs akimbo and her tiny front paws on her hips. 'Sterling chap. I was the base mascot and used to live with him – until he was posted overseas and Eddie kindly offered me a billet here.'

'Well, I'll be happy to give you a little fly-around on me back, if you like,' Stanley offered cheerfully. He'd heard Bunty's RAF stories on many occasions. 'Just grab a pawful of feathers, hang on tight and off we'll go.'

'That's very decent of you, old thing,' Bunty replied heartily. 'I've got a pair of flying goggles that used to belong to a doll knocking about somewhere. I'll root 'em out if I'm going to take to the air. Might need to lose a little ballast first, though,' she added, patting her round little belly and laughing.

'Hey, you two!' one of the goldfish shouted, jumping up out of the water of his tank and hanging over the side. 'Flying is for budgies. Real men travel on water, by ship.'

'Yeah, you tell 'em, Jake,' the other fish agreed, leaping up to join his brother. 'Me and Jake have travelled the South China Seas with pirates. Rough, tough, bloodcurdling pirates,' he boasted. 'You don't see the likes of them serving butties and tea and mopping up sick on one of them airy planes, do you?'

'No, you don't, Dan,' Jake agreed. 'Anyway, it would be very hard for a pirate to get down the aisle with teapots and things. All the pirates we know have wooden legs and hooks for hands, so they'd probably spill the tea.'

The fish certainly had vivid imaginations and, for the first time that day, their antics made Eddie laugh out loud, completely forgetting the pain of his cut lip. He could think of nothing better than sitting in his room, chatting away in private to his Amazing Animal Gang.

The fish were really going for it now and so, putting that niggling little worry he had about Dad's news firmly to the back of his mind, he settled back to hear what else Dan and Jake had to say on the subject of flying versus sailing.

CHAPTER SIX

'Yes, indeed,' Dan the goldfish gurgled, having just dropped back into the tank for a gulp of water. 'Give me a life sailing the Seven Seas any day, rather than flapping around in the sky. No, siree, if you ask me, flying is strictly for the birds.'

'How very observant of you,' Stanley sniffed. 'But, since the invention of the aeroplane, you'll find quite a few humans flying through the skies to destinations all over the world, as well as us birds. Although I have to say – we did it first.'

'Although there are flying fish,' Eddie added. 'There's loads of them in . . . erm . . .'

'Wigan?' Bunty offered.

'No, Barbados,' Stanley corrected her. 'Barbados is known as the land of the flying fish. Apparently, there's more fish flying about than birds.'

'Well, we've never seen any,' Dan replied sulkily, 'and we've sailed the Seven Seas.'

'As well as swimming in them. Don't forget that, Dan,' Jake added.

'Can I ask you something, boys?' Stanley asked. 'If you were pirates, how did you end up in a tank with fifty or so other goldfish in Fred's Aquatics?'

'Are you calling us liars?' a furious Dan exploded. 'I'll tell you how we ended up there. Our ship was scuttled and sunk by a band of Her Majesty's pirate-hunters, and Jake and me were cast into the sea and left swimming for ages and ages.'

'Yeah, months and months we were splashing about,' his brother added. 'Dodging sharks and poisonous jellyfish.'

'Then we were saved, but our rescuers turned out to be rival pirates who sold us to the evil Fred on the high street. So there, birdbrain,' Dan said, spitting a stream of water straight

at Stanley . . . but missing him. Instead, he caught Butch – who'd crawled back out from under the bed – right in the ear, which set him off barking angrily.

'I keel you,' he growled furiously. 'I tip

34

you down the toilet and then it's *adios, amigos.*'

'Calm down, Butch,' Eddie said, laughing. 'And the boys really are pirates,' he told Stanley with a big wink. 'Really scary pirates.'

'See?' the fish cried out in unison. 'Told you so.'

'Well, I don't believe it,' a grumpy Butch grumbled, scratching his damp ear with his hind paw. 'Not one word of it.'

'How do you think I lost my eye, then?' Dan demanded, pointing to a large dark stain over his right eye that looked remarkably like a black eyepatch and certainly gave him a swashbuckling air. 'I lost it in a sword fight with a member of the Chang Gang in Old Shanghai harbour.'

'It's a birthmark, not an eyepatch,' Butch said, growing bored now and finding the sock he'd discovered under Eddie's bed far more interesting. 'But, if you say you're pirates, then you're pirates. End of story.'

'Good,' the fish replied in unison again. 'So button your lip and mind your own business.' And they vanished back into the water with a double plop.

Everyone laughed at the spunky little fish apart from Butch, who was still annoyed at having water squirted in his ear and was now taking it out on Eddie's sock by worrying it.

'Oh well, chaps,' Bunty said. 'Don't wish to sound rude but if you don't mind I'm off to do a few hundred revolutions on my wheel before dinner.'

However, that niggling little worry that Eddie had briefly forgotten about rose to the surface again. Maybe Bunty could shed some light on what his dad was going to tell him.

'Before you do, Bunty,' Eddie said, 'I want to ask you something. Did you overhear Dad talking on the phone to anyone? Only he said he had some important news to tell me.'

'No, dear, I'm afraid I didn't as I was napping a bit today,' Bunty replied. 'I didn't sleep well last night. New straw, you see. It's always a bit scratchy at first.'

'Well, I've heard nothing because I wasn't here,' Stanley said. 'I was on the roof of the library discussing shiny things with a magpie called Maggie.'

The fish were sulking behind a clump of water plants so it was no good asking them, Eddie turned to Butch to see if he knew anything.

'Well, *chico*, I did hear something,' he offered reluctantly.

'What?' Eddie asked, keen to know. 'What did you hear?'

Butch lowered his voice. 'I heard him say something about

having to go away. Then someone your dad hadn't heard from in a long time rang up. They spoke for ages and it sounded like he was sending you to live with an ant.'

'An ant!' everyone shouted.

'Yes, an ant,' Butch went on. 'Can you believe it? An ant! Does that mean you'll be living under a paving stone or in a hole in the ground?'

'What about us?' Bunty thundered, getting into a bit of a fluster. 'Are we to be packed off with you to live with this ant? I'm afraid I'd rather stay here and starve than live with an insect!'

'Calm down,' Eddie said. 'They obviously meant an aunt, which is spelt A U N T. It means a female relation and not a tiny little ant. Honestly, get real, gang.'

'Of course, I knew exactly what your father meant by an aunt,' Stanley said haughtily. 'I'm an educated bird. But just who is this aunt?'

'And where does she live?' Bunty asked.

'I don't know,' Eddie told them, sitting back down on the bed with Butch on his knee. 'There's my Aunty Carol, but Dad doesn't get on with her, and anyway she lives in Australia and Dad couldn't afford the fare. I don't know what's going on, but whatever it is it doesn't sound good.'

They all remained silent for a moment, waiting for Eddie to speak.

'I'll find out when we're having our dinner,' he said. 'But wherever it is, gang, I'm not going anywhere without you lot.'

CHAPTER SEVEN

Eddie's parents were musicians, or at least they had been. They met when they were both working in the orchestra of a musical that was touring Europe. Eddie's dad could play the saxophone, the guitar and the piano, while his mum played the harp and the violin and had a beautiful singing voice.

They got married and a year later Eddie came along. Eddie's mum gave up touring to sing jingles on the radio and work as a backing singer, providing these jobs were close to home and didn't interfere with looking after Eddie. His dad still toured but only took on work that didn't keep him away from home for very long. They lived in a comfortable little house with a back garden and were very happy.

But when Eddie was four his mum became sick. She no longer lay next to him on his bed and sang him to sleep every night and he couldn't understand why. Then she was taken away in an ambulance and she never came home again.

Eddie had started to talk at a very early age, and his mum used to call him her little chatterbox. But, after she died, he stopped speaking entirely. For a long time he never uttered a word as, somewhere in the back of his mind, he wondered if his constant talking had been responsible for driving her away.

Now he was a single parent, Eddie's dad had given up being a musician so he could look after Eddie. He no longer played any instruments. Music reminded him of his wife and his grief was unbearable.

At first Eddie's dad had found it hard to get a job, because he wasn't trained to do anything but play music. He went from one poorly paid job to another until eventually he couldn't afford the mortgage on the house, and they were forced to move to a rented flat in the not-very-nice area where they were living now. But at least Eddie's dad had managed to find a permanent job working in a supermarket.

If you're wondering when Eddie started speaking again and how he discovered that he could communicate with animals, then I'll tell you. It happened during a visit to the zoo when he was around six years old. He was staring at the penguins in their enclosure and clearly heard one of them say to him, 'I'm so fed up.'

Without thinking, Eddie asked the penguin why he was fed up.

'Sick of fish, sick of swimming around in the same old pool and sick of this lot,' the penguin moaned, pointing a flipper in the direction of the other penguins, who were either sitting on the rocks in groups or splashing about as they jumped into the concrete pool. 'No ambition, that's their problem,' the penguin said, shaking his head. 'Whereas I fully intend to travel to Cape Town in South Africa to visit my relatives.'

'How are you going to get there?' Eddie asked, surprised to hear his own voice again after so long.

'Easy. I intend to catch the bus,' the penguin replied grandly, 'and I shall take a packed lunch of sardines for the journey.' With that, he waddled away.

Eddie's dad was amused at the sight of a penguin screeching and honking at Eddie and the boy answering back as if he understood every word it was saying. He was also over the moon to hear his son speak again, as he'd been growing extremely worried about him. He thought it was cute and very funny that Eddie should choose to speak to a penguin, but he didn't have a clue that his son could really and truly understand everything the bird was saying and genuinely hold a conversation with it.

Since then Eddie's talents had developed, and talking to animals – who all have their own individual personalities, as it turns out – became as natural as talking to humans. But from an early age he'd realised that his ability was highly unusual, so he kept it to himself.

The kitchen was full of smoke, as it quite often was when Eddie's dad was cooking.

'Phew,' Eddie said, waving the smoke away from his face. 'Open the window, Dad, or you'll set the smoke alarm off again.'

'We're having rissoles tonight,' his dad said cheerfully as he opened the window to let the smoke out. 'I got them half price.'

As they sat eating their meal, Eddie kept waiting for the moment his dad was going to break whatever news he had in store for him.

'Eddie,' his dad said eventually, standing up and going to the tap to get a drink of water. 'There's something I have to talk to you about.'

Here it comes, Eddie thought, *the bad news. Well, let's hear it, then.*

'The company are offering me a promotion. They think I'm management material,' he explained. 'It'll mean a lot more responsibility and I wonder if I'm up for it . . . but, if I do take them up on their offer, it means I'll have to go away on a training course for three weeks.'

'Can't I come with you?' Eddie asked anxiously. 'I won't get in the way.'

'Much as I'd love you to come with me, I'm afraid you can't,' Dad explained kindly. 'The course is in Middlesbrough and I'll be staying in a bed and breakfast. What would you do all day stuck in a room in a strange town without your animals? I doubt the B & B allows pets. No, I'm sorry, son, but it just wouldn't work.'

'So what's going to happen to me, then?' Eddie said, feeling very worried now.

'I had a phone call today from someone I hadn't heard from since the funeral,' Dad said, sitting down again. 'Did you ever hear me or your mum mention Aunt Budge?'

'No,' said Eddie.

'She's your mum's aunty,' his dad explained. 'She married an archaeologist and spent all her time away in Egypt and various other faraway places, digging up ancient artefacts. She hadn't been seen for years until she turned up for your mother's funeral. Your mum was very fond of Aunt Budge, and the old girl wrote to me a lot after the funeral, but I wasn't in a good place at the time and never responded. Then you and I moved to this flat, and we just lost touch.'

'Well, how did she find out where we are now, then?' Eddie asked.

'Uncle Jack told her. He was a musician at the time.'

Aunt Budge had gone through a terrible time, apparently, trapped for quite a while between two war-torn countries in the Middle East, where she'd helped out by driving a lorry loaded with medical supplies for the injured. After such a hair-raising, not to mention dangerous experience, Aunt Budge had decided to pamper herself a little. She certainly deserved it and so she had travelled from country to country, visiting old friends, until she found herself in a beautiful suite of rooms at Raffles Hotel in Singapore.

As she was leaving the hotel one day to buy a hat, she'd bumped into Eddie's Uncle Jack, who was playing at a club in town and was visiting the hotel for one of their famous curries. They remembered each other from Eddie's mum's funeral so Jack had asked her to join him for an early lunch in the Tiffin

44

Room, which she did. They'd had a long, long chat over a very hot curry.

'Anyway, it's really great that she's got in touch, as I'm quite fond of her,' Eddie's dad said. 'She's a lady, you know.'

'Well, I didn't think she was a man,' Eddie replied.

'No, I mean she's got a title. Her late husband, who died some time ago, was Lord Reginald Sprockett. That makes your Aunt Budge Lady Buddleia Sprockett.'

'Oh,' was all Eddie could think of saying, as he really wasn't that interested in some old relative he'd never met. He was more concerned about what was going to happen to him while Dad was away.

'So . . . what do you think of this idea?' Dad said hesitantly. 'I was talking to her for quite some time – she could talk the hind leg off a donkey – and I told her about the promotion and how I had to go away, and she asked if you'd like to go and stay with her.'

'Um…' said Eddie nervously. 'But I don't know her. Where does she live?'

'Well, she doesn't really have a permanent home because she travels around so much, but at the moment she's staying in her "little house", as she put it, in Amsterdam.'

'Amsterdam in Holland?' Eddie couldn't believe his ears. Go all the way to Holland to stay with an old lady in a tiny house? Had his dad gone mad? 'What about Butch and Bunty and the fish? What'll happen to them? And how would I even get to Amsterdam?'

Eddie had a million and one questions and, after Dad had calmed him down, he explained the plan. Aunt Budge loved animals and would welcome Eddie's animal gang. Travel permits would be no problem for them because Aunt Budge was well connected and knew people who could arrange such things – all very above board and legal, of course. Her chauffeur would pick Eddie up from the flat and drive him and the animals to Amsterdam. Of course, all this would depend on whether Eddie was happy to go.

'At least think about it,' his dad said. 'Amsterdam is a beautiful city and it'll be a change for you. If I go on the course and get this promotion, it'll mean much better pay, which means we'll be able to get out of this place and find somewhere better to live. So . . . any thoughts?'

Eddie simply nodded, which could've meant anything.

'Now, go and do your homework,' his dad said, 'and if you finish it then I'll let you play on my computer for a bit. Off you go.'

Eddie went into his bedroom. Closing the door slowly behind him, he leant on it and stared silently at the animals.

'Well?' they demanded. 'What's happening?'

Eddie was enjoying keeping them in suspense, but to their relief he eventually spoke.

'Pack your bags,' he said. 'We're going to Amsterdam.'

CHAPTER EIGHT

'Amsterdam?' Butch exclaimed. He was sitting on the roof of Bunty's doll's house, which she wasn't very happy about. But he simply ignored her anxious demands for him to get down and remained where he was.

'Rude little dog,' Bunty said in a huff. 'Serves him right if he falls.'

'So, Amsterdam, aye? Well, that is a turn-up for the books,' Stanley said. 'And would this be to stay with the mysterious aunty, by any chance?'

'Yes, she's got a little house over there,' Eddie said. 'But I'm not happy about having to live with some ancient old aunty in an ancient old house that probably smells of cats. Plus, I imagine she'll make me go to bed really early. The good news, though, is that you can all come with me. She's arranging special travel permits for you.'

'Hang about, *chico*. Let's go back a bit. Did you just mention cats?' Butch asked, having just realised what Eddie had said. 'You did, didn't you? You said the house will smell of cats and that means she must have one. Well, bring it on,' he growled angrily, ''cos I'm going to run it out of town.'

'Actually, I'm not overkeen on cats, either, for obvious reasons,' Bunty agreed nervously, her tiny face wrinkled with worry. 'Perhaps I'd better stay here.'

'Listen to yourselves,' Stanley exclaimed, hopping back on to the windowsill from the desk. 'You've been given the chance of a lifetime to travel somewhere new and all you can do is moan and worry about cats.'

'Can you blame me?' Bunty protested. 'They do terrible things to hamsters! They like to play with us but we certainly don't want to play with them.'

'And fish,' Dan and Jake cried, hanging over the side of their tank. 'But we ain't scared of no cat. We've fought tigers.'

'Don't worry, *amigos*,' Butch announced. 'I'll defend you all. The cat will have to go.'

'Will you stop?' Stanley said firmly. 'You don't even know if there is a cat yet, so calm down. And Bunty,' he added craftily, 'don't you realise that Amsterdam is where hamsters originated?'

Bunty snorted. 'Nonsense,' she said. 'The first ever sighting of a hamster was in Syria.'

'Yes, but before that they lived in Holland,' Stanley informed her. 'I'm surprised you didn't know that, being such a well-read hamster.'

Butch sniggered when he heard this, but Bunty simply ignored him. 'Please carry on with this fascinating story, Stanley,' she simpered, giving Butch a dirty look.

'Long, long ago, way back in the old days, Amsterdam was originally known as *Hamster*dam,' Stanley told her, winking a beady eye at Eddie.

'Really?' Bunty exclaimed, her eyes widening.

'Amsterdam was populated by millions of hamsters at one time, which is why they named it Hamsterdam,' the sly bird replied. 'The H was dropped after a load of Cockney hamsters from the East End of London moved there, so *Hamsterdam* became *Amsterdam* due to their accents.'

'Well, tickle my tail with a feather,' Bunty gasped. 'In that case, I'll just have to go to Hamsterdam and discover my roots, cat or no cat. What say you all? Are you with me?'

 Eddie laughed as they all cheered, and suddenly the prospect of three weeks

in Hamsterdam didn't seem so bad.

'Right, let's get your maths homework sorted and then I'm off,' Stanley announced. 'I've got a hot date later.'

The homework turned out to be very tricky, but with Stanley's help Eddie sort of got the hang of fractions, which would please Miss Taylor no end when he handed it in tomorrow.

'Now that's finished, can I get on with me night?' he asked Eddie. 'Am I looking hot or what? Feathers all in place? Got a nice sheen to them? Beak nice and shiny? Then open the window and let me show my date what a good time looks like.'

Eddie watched as the bird flew over the neighbouring rooftops. Yawning loudly, he realised he was pretty sleepy. So, after taking Butch out for a quick walk round the block, he cleaned his teeth, put his PJs on and shouted goodnight to his dad in the front room.

'No computer games, then?' Dad shouted back.

'Too sleepy,' Eddie replied.

'Made your mind up about your aunty yet?' his dad asked.

'Yes,' Eddie said, yawning loudly. 'I'll go to Amsterdam.'

'Good lad.' His dad sounded both relieved and happy. 'I'll ring her in the morning.'

Once in bed, with Butch at his side, Eddie lay staring at the constellation of plastic glow-in-the-dark stars that Dad had stuck on the ceiling to hide a damp patch. He was going to miss his bedroom, where he felt safe surrounded by all his important bits and pieces that were so familiar to him.

Butch growled sleepily. 'Cats,' Eddie heard him mutter. 'I'll run 'em out of town.'

'Go to sleep, cowboy,' Eddie said, yawning loudly again and turning over in bed. 'And, if she has got a moggy, then you'd better leave it alone.'

Butch growled again and said a rude word.

CHAPTER NINE

The end of term came round far too quickly for Eddie. He'd been looking forward to the summer holidays, but now he wasn't so sure. Dad had already packed his holdall for the trip to Middlesbrough and now he was packing a case for Eddie's trip to Amsterdam.

'You've got lots of underpants,' he said, doing his best to fold some clothes neatly but not having much success. 'And I've put your suit in, with a shirt and tie.'

'But I haven't worn that in ages,' Eddie protested. 'It'll be too small for me now.'

'Don't talk daft, of course it'll fit,' his dad said. 'You might need it, just in case you go somewhere nice.'

Eddie sighed as he sat on the bed, listening to his dad rattle on. He could just imagine what the 'somewhere nice' would be. Tea parties with a load of old ladies, flower-arranging displays and long, boring sessions in a cold church listening to one doddery old Dutchman giving a classical recital while another old fossil accompanied him on an out-of-tune organ.

'Don't forget to polish your shoes,' Dad went on, 'and change your socks and clean your teeth and flush the toilet when you do a number two.'

'I always do,' Eddie protested. 'I always flush.'

'Make sure you do. You don't want your poor old aunty walking into the bathroom and finding a dirty big poo staring at her.'

'Dad!' Eddie shouted, squirming with embarrassment. 'I'm not a little kid.'

'Yes, you are,' Dad said, ruffling his hair. 'You're my little man and I'm going to miss you something shocking. Give your old dad a kiss.'

'Dad . . . ' Eddie said again, squirming even more and blushing an even deeper red. 'That's not cool. I'm going into the front room to watch telly.'

As he flicked through the channels to try and find a programme that wasn't a quiz show or someone telling you how to cook, he could hear Dad talking on his phone in the kitchen.

'Righty-ho,' he was saying. 'Ten o'clock tomorrow morning

it is. He's all ready to go. Speak soon. Cheerio.'

Eddie suddenly developed butterflies in his stomach. So that was it, then. At ten o'clock tomorrow morning, he'd be shipped off to somewhere in Amsterdam, probably never to be seen again.

'That was your aunt,' his dad said, coming into the front room. 'She's sending her chauffeur to pick you up in the morning. You'll be driving all the way to Amsterdam. Exciting, isn't it?'

'Yes,' Eddie replied in a flat, miserable voice. 'Dead exciting.'

'Now, don't be like that, Eddie,' Dad said reproachfully. 'Your aunt is a very interesting woman. She's travelled all over the world and she's a remarkable archaeologist.'

Eddie grunted as he pictured a house stuffed with bits of old rock and stone heads with no noses.

'I guarantee you'll have a wonderful time,' his dad was saying. 'Just don't tire her out because she's got to be very old now. Keep the noise down.'

Eddie sighed. Could things get any worse?

CHAPTER TEN

The next morning Eddie felt sick with dread. Today was the big day and he'd woken up really early after a restless sleep. He'd spent half the night awake, wondering what was going to happen to him. Now, he was busy packing his holdall with what he called personal things – his journal and a notebook, a selection of pens and pencils, a compass, his passport, the animals' travel documents, a travelling alarm clock, a small jar of fish food, his savings (£8.11, kept safe inside a pencil case) and Ruby, an ancient teddy bear with an ear missing. He didn't care if his aunt thought it babyish to be sleeping with a teddy bear at his age. He'd had Ruby for as long as he could remember and he wasn't going anywhere without her – and that was that.

Bunty was checking out the living quarters in her travel cage, and the fish were sulking because Eddie had transferred them to a much smaller tank with a lid full of air holes so they didn't splash water all over the car. Butch was admiring his new coat in the wardrobe mirror.

'Not bad,' he said, turning round so he could get a good look at his rear end. 'But I don't know why I couldn't wear my poncho.'

'Because Dad said it looked scruffy and he wanted you to make a good impression – that's why,' Eddie said as he zipped up his holdall.

'Huh,' Butch replied. 'But Mexican bandits don't wear tartan coats, do they? Someone should tell him.'

'You know, if the wind's good, then I might fly over and pay you a visit,' Stanley remarked, sitting in his usual position on the windowsill. 'I could do with a little holiday.' Suddenly, he let out a long whistle. 'Boy, oh boy, oh boy,' he said. 'Wait until you see this beauty sitting outside the house.'

'What is it?' Eddie asked.

'Probably some lady crow he's seen,' Butch remarked absently, still preoccupied with his new coat.

Eddie scrambled over his bed to take a look out of the window . . . and gasped when he saw the car parked outside.

'Wow!' was all he could say as he stared, open-mouthed, at the most beautiful car he'd ever seen. It was long and sleek.

The bonnet was a deep red while the bodywork was cream. Every bit of chrome-work on this motor gleamed like polished silver and it left Eddie speechless.

'It's a vintage Bentley coupé,' Stanley said knowledgeably, just as impressed as Eddie. 'Just look at it – pure elegance and class. I wonder who it belongs to?'

All around, curtains were twitching as the neighbours took a peek at the magnificent vehicle that stood out like a bird of paradise among all the other mundane and boring cars parked in the road.

From out of it stepped a very tall, very thin and very old man. He was wearing a peaked cap and a dark blue uniform. To Eddie's surprise, he opened the gate, walked up to the front door and rang the bell.

'It's your aunty's driver,' Stanley exclaimed excitedly. 'That car's come for you!'

Eddie snapped out of his gloomy mood, excitement tingling all over him. 'Wow!' was all he could say – again – and then he rushed to the front door.

'I'm Whetstone, Lady Sprockett's chauffeur, sir,' the tall man was saying to Eddie's dad. 'I've come to pick the boy up as requested.'

'Well, here he is, right on cue,' Eddie's dad replied. 'And looking a lot more cheerful than he did earlier on, I might say.'

Eddie had never been away from his dad before, especially for so long, and now that the time had come to say goodbye

he suddenly felt very lonely. There was a lump in his throat that felt like he'd swallowed a golf ball, and he tried desperately to hold back the tears as he gave him a hug. What would he do if something terrible happened to Dad in Middlesbrough, wherever that was? Eddie might end up living with his aunt, who no doubt would pack him off to a boarding school in the wilds of Scotland. He'd have to get up at six a.m. and go for a long run whatever the weather, and when he got back he'd have to face cold showers and lumpy porridge.

'Chin up, little man,' Dad said as Eddie embraced him. 'I'll be back in no time. By then you might not even want to come home.'

'Are you joking?' Eddie said, trying to swallow but the golf ball was in the way. 'I don't want to go in the first place.'

His dad laughed and gave him a wink. 'We'll see,' was all he said.

Quite a crowd had gathered to take a look at the car. Even Mr Ali's cat had put in an appearance. Everyone was keen to see who such a vehicle had come for.

Inside, the car was all creamy leather upholstery and shiny wood. It smelt very expensive and new.

'Beautiful. It's like being in a meringue. White on the outside and lovely chewy toffee on the inside,' Eddie heard Bunty say from her travelling cage as he climbed into his seat.

'Well, don't start chewing the woodwork or the seats,'

Eddie warned. 'Anyway, how do you know what meringue tastes like?'

'I wouldn't dream of chewing the furnishings,' Bunty replied haughtily. 'As for the meringue . . . well, there was a tea party in the officers' mess once and I sneaked across the table and nibbled my way inside one. Mmmm, heaven,' she added dreamily.

Butch was delighted to have a crowd of neighbours peering inside the car at him and he leapt up and down on the seat, yapping excitedly.

'Yeah, baby!' he was shouting to Mrs King who lived next door. She was tapping on the window and waving. 'We're going to live with the Queen,' he yapped.

The fish were still sulking in silence.

'Have you fastened your seat belt?' Whetstone asked as he started the car. 'Because, if you're ready, sir, we'd best go. Wouldn't want to miss the train.'

Eddie waved to his dad and the car pulled away. He could feel the golf ball in his throat turning into a rugby ball as he watched his dad vanish from sight.

However, the ball quickly and miraculously disappeared when the car turned smoothly round the corner. For there, holding an ice cream and rooted to the spot in shock, was Quentin, his eyes almost bulging out of his head. The boy's mouth looked capable of housing a bird and a nest of chicks, it was open so wide. He seemed awestruck at the sight of Eddie sitting in the back of this beautiful car.

Eddie waved cheerily and shouted, 'See ya!', even though he knew Quentin couldn't hear him.

Quentin was so amazed he allowed his hand to droop. The enormous, barely licked swirl of vanilla with a chocolate flake and sprinkles slid off its cone and hit the pavement with a loud splat.

He wasn't quite sure what upset him the most – losing his

 ice cream that he hadn't even had a tiny little lick of, now slowing melting on the pavement, or the sight of Eddie sitting in the back of that unbelievably magnificent car.

Maybe a charity is taking poor kids out for the day, he told himself as he set off for home with a face like thunder. *Or maybe his dad has won the lottery.* Quentin stopped in his tracks, horrified at the thought that Eddie's dad might suddenly be extremely wealthy.

'No way,' he muttered angrily to himself. 'There's no way that Eddie Albert's dad can be richer than my dad. That just can't happen.' Allowing his temper to get the better of him, he kicked the wall hard, hurting his big toe in the process and letting out a yowl of pain.

'That's Eddie Albert's fault,' he moaned as he hopped about. 'He made me do it.'

With that, he limped home, feeling very sorry for himself.

CHAPTER ELEVEN

E ddie, on the other hand, suddenly felt quite cheerful.

Having let herself out of her travelling compartment, as she liked to call it, Bunty was investigating her surroundings. 'Beautiful vehicle,' she remarked. 'Reminds me of a similar automobile that the air chief marshal travelled in when he visited the base.'

'What were you doing in the car of such a high-ranking officer?' Butch asked jealously, curious to know how a humble hamster had managed to hitch a ride in such a fabulous car.

'As you know, I was the regimental mascot,' she replied proudly, 'and therefore entitled to such privileges due to my rank and station.'

'Oh.' Butch yawned, bored stiff at the thought of being trapped in a car and having to listen to another long-winded tale of Bunty's life in the RAF. He turned quickly away from her and pressed his nose against the window, staring out idly, his warm breath making a fifty-pence-piece-sized patch of steam on the glass.

'What's my aunty like, Mr Whetstone?' Eddie asked the chauffeur. 'You see, I've never met her. Is she nice?'

'Nice?' Whetstone spluttered, obviously amused by this, judging by the way he chuckled to himself. 'I'd say she was more . . .' He paused as he struggled to find a suitable word to describe Lady Buddleia.

'More what?' Eddie urged, anxious to know.

'More . . . like this car,' Whetstone wheezed, still laughing. 'She's unique. Anyway, you'll soon meet her and then you can judge for yourself.'

'Thanks, Mr Whetstone,' Eddie said. If this magnificent car was anything to go by, he suspected his aunt was truly unique.

'If the motorway's clear, we'll be at the tunnel in no time,' Whetstone said, looking at Eddie's reflection in the rear-view mirror. 'And, by the way, there's no need to call me mister. Just plain old Whetstone will do. Now, sit back, young sir, and enjoy the ride.'

It was exciting to drive on to a train at Folkestone, go through an enormous tunnel underneath the English Channel and come out at Calais in France thirty-five minutes later.

'Welcome to France, young Eddie,' Whetstone said. 'Now it's a nice straight road all the way to Holland.'

They drove through France and into Belgium, stopping off at Ghent to refuel and stretch their legs. When they got stuck in some heavy traffic at Antwerp, Eddie, who hadn't had much sleep the night before, started to doze. Eventually, he fell into a deep sleep with Butch on his knee. The dog had also nodded off and was snoring loudly.

Eddie had a peculiar dream that he was looking for someone without being quite sure who it was. He kept knocking on people's doors and calling, 'Are you there?' through the letterbox.

Finally, he crawled into a long dark tunnel and heard a voice shouting, 'We're here!'

'Where?' he kept asking but the voice just repeated, 'We're here. Wake up, we're here.'

He woke with a shock and for a moment didn't know where he was.

'Wake up, Mr Eddie,' Whetstone was saying. 'We're here. We've arrived in Amsterdam.'

Eddie sat up quickly and looked out of the window. The

first thing he thought was, *Where are all the windmills?* There were lots of shops with signs above them written in a language that he couldn't understand, and everyone seemed to be riding a bike. Eddie's had been stolen from outside a shop a few months ago and he really missed cycling to school. Maybe he could borrow a bike, or even rent one while he was here, if they weren't too expensive. He'd ask his aunt as she was bound to know.

Church bells were ringing out, the beautiful melodic chimes playing a tune that Eddie thought he'd heard somewhere before. 'Those bells sound like a Beatles song,' he said to Whetstone.

'You're right,' Whetstone replied. 'That's the *Westerkerk*. Those old church bells play all sorts of tunes. Did you know that kerk is Dutch for church?'

They turned into a long street called *Keizersgracht*, where Aunt Budge lived. All Eddie could say when he saw the long, tall, elegant houses overlooking the canal was, 'Wow, it's beautiful!'

'It certainly is,' Whetstone agreed. 'These are the famous canal houses of Old Amsterdam,' he explained, slowing down to let a group of cyclists past. 'They've been there a long time.

Your aunt's house was built in 1667, one year after the Great Fire of London.'

'Wow,' Eddie said again.

After driving over a small hump back bridge with what looked like hundreds of bicycles chained to the railings, they finally arrived outside Aunt Budge's house.

'This is it,' Whetstone said. 'Are you ready to meet your aunt?'

CHAPTER TWELVE

The car had pulled up outside one of the bigger houses. Eddie stood and counted the number of floors as Whetstone unloaded the car. There were six in total, including the basement, and it all looked very grand. Nothing like the little house his aunt had described to Dad over the phone.

The basement door suddenly opened and a small, highly excitable lady burst out of the kitchen beyond. She was wearing a large white apron, her hair was wrapped up in a scarf and on her feet were a pair of battered old trainers. She was also covered in flour.

Rushing at Eddie, she gave him a bear hug that took his breath away. As she squeezed him tightly, he could see little clouds of flour floating off her.

This must be the cook, Eddie thought as he tried to peel her off him. And a very friendly cook at that.

'I'm Eddie,' he said timidly, once the cook had let go of him. 'Is my aunt in? She knows I'm coming. I'm her nephew.'

The cook roared with laughter. Pulling off her headscarf, she shouted, 'I am your Aunt Budge! Who did you think I was? One of the staff?'

Highly embarrassed, Eddie just grinned.

'Oh, my dear, give your aunt a kiss,' she said, beaming like a lighthouse and pulling Eddie towards her again. 'It's lovely to meet you,' she gushed. 'My, how you remind me of your dear mother. Same blond hair and big blue eyes. I had no idea you were so handsome.'

Eddie blushed a deep red.

'Thank you, Your Majesty,' he replied, bowing his head slightly, aware that his dad had said she was a titled lady.

'Please, my dear,' Aunt Budge implored. 'I am certainly not royalty and I'm only a lady by marriage. You see, my late husband, your Uncle Reginald, was a lord by birth and when we married I automatically became a lady. Very posh,' she added, giving Eddie a wink. 'Now, come on into the kitchen – I've baked a cake! – and bring your adorable pets as I'm dying to meet them. Whetstone will unload the car and take your things up to your room. I've put you in the attic – I know you'll love it. Did you have a good trip?' she asked Whetstone. 'No bumps or scrapes or speeding tickets, I hope? Good. Now, come this way, Eddie. Two steps down, so mind your head.'

The kitchen was large with a stone-flagged floor. It was also nice and cool, out of the late-afternoon sun. If it hadn't been for the big cooking range and the huge fridge, Eddie thought they could have been in another century.

Butch was mooching round the kitchen, sniffing underneath the large oak cupboards to see if there was anything interesting to chew on. Eddie put Bunty's travelling compartment next to the fish tank, which he'd placed on top of a small cabinet.

'Pssst!' Bunty hissed from behind the mesh on the flap of her door. 'Ask if she's got a cat.'

'No, we haven't,' Aunt Budge said automatically.

'Haven't what?' Eddie asked.

'Got a cat,' Aunt Budge replied.

'But I never asked if you had a cat . . .' a stunned Eddie exclaimed, his voice trailing off.

Aunt Budge seemed flustered all of a sudden. 'Isn't that what you were going to ask me?' she asked in a slightly higher-pitched voice. 'I just thought that what with the dog, the hamster and the fish, the first thing you'd want to know is if I had a cat. Now, I'll just put a bowl of water out for that dear little dog and see if I haven't got a few nuts for the hamster.'

'Oh, don't worry about us,' Jake moaned from inside their temporary tank. 'We'll just sit here in this plastic box like an exhibit at an art gallery.'

'As for those two little fish,' Aunt Budge said as she placed a bowl of water on the floor, 'there's a nice big tank in one of the spare rooms. I'll get Whetstone to dig it out. It's got all the filters and things, and I'm sure that the fish would be a lot happier in it.'

Eddie was puzzled. Had Aunt Budge heard what Jake said or was it just a coincidence that she mentioned the tank? And what about Bunty and the cat? Had she heard and understood the hamster?

No, she really couldn't have, he told himself. *It must've been a coincidence.*

'You're earlier than I expected,' Aunt Budge was saying as she flitted round the kitchen. 'Which explains why I'm not suitably dressed. Whetstone wasn't speeding, was he? He does have a tendency to put his foot down. I keep telling him: just because the sign says sixty miles an hour, it doesn't mean it's compulsory to drive at that speed.'

She kept up this incessant stream of chatter as she darted round the kitchen, picking things up and putting them down again. 'I'm afraid my cook will come home early. She's Bavarian and excellent at her job, but she absolutely forbids me to go anywhere near her kitchen. Yes, *her* kitchen, she calls it, but what can I do? She says I'm messy and I leave the place looking like an absolute tip, which of course is just plain drivel, but I daren't argue because she's so bossy.'

Looking round at the general clutter, the chaos of bowls and pans, and the broken egg on the table that was dripping on to the spilt flour, Eddie thought Aunt Budge's cook might have a valid point.

'Lady Buddleia . . .' he said, trying to get a word in edge-ways.

'Oh, please,' she replied quickly, 'don't call me that. It makes me sound like I should be wearing a big hat and opening a village fête.'

'Well, what shall I call you, then? Eddie asked.

'I'll tell you what,' Aunt Budge said, moving a bowl with a big wooden spoon in it off a chair so she could sit down. 'When I was a girl, my younger sister couldn't pronounce "Buddleia" – which, by the way, is a most unsuitable name for anything but a plant – so she called me Budgie, which eventually became Budge. All the family – what's left of them, that is – call me Budge, so why don't you?'

'Okey-dokey,' Eddie said, grinning. 'Aunt Budge it is.'

'Excellent,' she pronounced. 'Let's go upstairs. I expect you'd like to freshen up after such a long journey so I'll show you to your room. Now, be warned: there are a lot of steps in this house and, apart from the staircase in the hall, they're extremely steep and narrow, as in all Dutch houses. I don't know how Cook manages with her big feet. Enormous they are, like a hobbit's—'

Aunt Budge stopped in mid-flow at the sight of a very large woman standing at the top of the stairs.

'What are you doing in my kitchen?' the large woman demanded. 'And with a dog as well?' She glowered at Butch, who growled at her in response.

'See what I mean?' Aunt Budge whispered out of the corner of her mouth. 'She thinks she owns the place.'

Eddie smiled.

'I was just baking a cake for my nephew here,' Aunt Budge said more loudly, and somewhat apologetically, 'and I can assure you that this sweet little dog is spotlessly clean. He belongs to my nephew. Allow me to introduce him – Eddie, this is Miss Schmidt, the best cook in Europe.' Aunt Budge added that last bit in order to flatter her, hoping she would overlook the mess in the kitchen.

Miss Schmidt nodded. 'Good to meet you,' she said to Eddie in a very deep voice.

'And the same to you,' Eddie replied with a cheesy grin.

'Could you tell me something, Lady B?' Miss Schmidt

asked with a grim expression on her face. 'What exactly is that burning smell coming from my kitchen?'

'The cake!' Aunt Budge screamed, rushing back down the stairs. 'I completely forgot.'

'Your aunt is a strange woman,' Miss Schmidt sighed as she followed Aunt Budge down the stairs. 'God help you and keep you safe, child.'

CHAPTER THIRTEEN

here was a bit of a fuss over the mess. Miss Schmidt
threatened to resign until Aunt Budge made a solemn
promise that she would never go into her kitchen again. Miss
Schmidt, somewhat mollified by this, set about tidying up and
making something to eat, muttering to herself angrily in her
native language as she sliced tomatoes.

They ate their lunch in what Aunt Budge called the
morning room. Apart from school trips to a museum and an
art gallery, Eddie had never been in such a grand room. It
had a very high ceiling with ornate carvings round the edge
and a magnificent crystal chandelier suspended from the
middle. There were three large windows with a long padded
seat underneath them looking out over the canal and down
to the street below. The walls of this room were covered in
hand-painted, pale-blue-and-yellow silk wallpaper and on
each one hung an assortment of imposing old paintings of

horses, stern men in uniform and miserable-looking women in big hats.

'My late husband's ancestors,' Aunt Budge explained, noticing that Eddie seemed interested in them. She waved a stick of celery around like a baton as she pointed each portrait out. 'That chap with the big moustache hanging over the writing desk is the Right Honourable Jasper Sprockett. He was an intrepid explorer who was unfortunately trampled by a rhino. And the rather fancy woman by the door is Lady Araminta Sprockett, my husband's great-great-great-aunt. The artist was inclined to flatter his subjects, which was certainly the case with Araminta as she certainly didn't have such luxurious hair as she does in her portrait, nor did she have such pearly white teeth. In fact, she was as bald as a hard-boiled egg and didn't have a tooth in her head.'

Eddie sniggered. Aunt Budge wasn't at all like the miserable old woman he'd thought she'd be. She was funny, lively and very interesting, and the house she'd described as 'little' was anything but. The animals had already been charmed by her. She'd placed the fish in their spacious new tank out of the sun but near the window, so they could still see the canal, and she'd insisted that Bunty be allowed to run freely round the room.

Butch was totally besotted with Aunt Budge and he now sat curled up on her lap with a contented grin on his face as she stroked his ears.

'Now then,' she announced after they'd finished eating, 'I suggest we take the boat out before it gets dark. I'm sure you'd enjoy a quick trip round the canals before we have our dinner.'

Aunt Budge kept a small electric-powered boat moored outside the house and in no time they were cruising down the canal with Bunty sitting in Eddie's shirt pocket, Butch hanging over the side, barking at the water, and Aunt Budge at the wheel wearing a sailor's cap.

Eddie was fascinated by the amount of traffic on the canal – the long tourist boats packed full of people enjoying the view, and teenagers pedalling away furiously on rented pedaloes as they tried unsuccessfully to travel in a straight line. There were party boats, boats with families enjoying a picnic on board, and one that carried a woman in a wedding dress who was waving at everyone. Eddie presumed she had just got married.

'I think it's time you took over at the helm,' Aunt Budge said after a while.

'Me?' Eddie asked, amazed that she'd trust him to steer a boat when he'd never done anything like that before.

'Well, I wasn't talking to Butch,' she replied, smiling. 'It's easy – just keep to the right going down and to the left coming back – big boats take precedence over small ones. Keep a nice slow, steady course . . . oh, and don't hit the houseboats.'

The next thing Eddie knew he was in charge of the boat and wearing Aunt Budge's sailor cap. After a minor scrape underneath a bridge and a tricky moment with a very large tourist vessel, he was soon sailing the canals like an old hand.

As he manoeuvred expertly under a bridge, he suddenly felt liberated, like he was capable of doing anything at all. To think that only this morning he'd been dreading coming to Amsterdam, and now here he was steering a boat down a canal! The happy feeling that glowed in Eddie's tummy told him there was a very good chance he might like it here.

CHAPTER FOURTEEN

O ver the next week or so, Eddie's feet didn't touch the ground as he seemed to spend most of his time cycling. The magnificent car never left the garage – Aunt Budge was a very enthusiastic cyclist and preferred to go everywhere by bike. Eddie's was just one of a collection that lived in the garden shed behind the house.

Whetstone had cleaned it and pumped up the tyres and, although it was a bit old-fashioned, Eddie zipped happily round the city on it. They cycled through the big park that Aunt Budge said was called the *Volderpark*, with Butch enjoying the ride in the basket on the front of Aunt Budge's bike.

They visited museums and art galleries and went to the flower market, and on Saturday morning Aunt Budge went shopping in the markets of the *Jordaan*. Normally, Eddie found shopping with his dad a bit of a bore, but the market in the *Jordaan* was an Aladdin's cave where, it seemed, you could find just about everything you ever wanted. There were stalls selling eggs and cheese, fresh bread and every variety of mushroom that ever existed. There were others piled high with fruit and vegetables and great mounds of fresh aromatic herbs. There were second-hand clothes, antiques and junk, old books, toys, huge bunches of flowers, ceramics, hats, candles, spices and delicious-looking pastries that Aunt Budge just couldn't resist. She bought a large raspberry tart and handed it to Whetstone, who was carrying the bags.

When Aunt Budge was satisfied she'd got everything she needed – as well as quite a few things she didn't need but 'just couldn't leave' – she sent Whetstone home with the mountain of shopping bags and took Eddie into a local café for some apple pie and a huge mug of hot chocolate.

Eddie was loving life in Amsterdam.

When they got home that Saturday morning, Aunt Budge reckoned that the two helpings of apple pie she'd wolfed down in the café had made her sleepy, so she excused herself to go for a lie-down. Butch was full of beans and Eddie thought that a walk might burn off some of his energy and stop him charging around the room.

As they were leaving the house, a girl who was sitting on the top step of the house next door gave a whistle. Eddie immediately looked up.

'Who are you?' she asked, staring at him.

'Who are you?' Eddie replied, thinking this girl was a bit rude.

'I asked first,' she said, shoving her hands into the pockets of her shorts.

'Well, I'm Eddie,' he told her. 'And who are you?'

'Floortje Anna Maria Antonia Uffen,' she said. 'But everyone calls me Flo. My mother is Brazilian and my father is Dutch.'

'Well, hello, Flo. Hey, that rhymes,' Eddie said, grinning.

Flo just looked at him as if she hadn't understood a word he'd said. 'Who is the old lady next door? Your grandmother?'

'No, she's my aunt.'

'She owns the whole house?'

'Yes.'

'We live in a flat at the top of our house.'

'Oh.'

'You live here now?' she asked.

'Yes, but just for a while during the school holidays.'

'You like your school? Have you got lots of friends at school?'

Eddie secretly thought that she asked a lot of questions. 'Well, I'm not exactly crazy about school,' he told her, 'and I don't really get on with the other kids.'

'That's just how I feel,' Flo agreed, jumping down from the top step. 'I go to a really weird school. They have chess competitions and stuff like that, which I don't care for at all, and my classmates are so booooooring, and sooooooo snobbish I don't bother with them. We have nothing at all in common. Every day is the same, every conversation is the same and I'm always being told off for not wearing my stupid hat outside school. Do you know,' she went on, 'they think I'm peculiar because I go to boxing classes. Why shouldn't girls box? It's soooooooooo boring. I just wish that something exciting would happen.'

'Like what?' Eddie asked.

'I dunno,' she said, shrugging her shoulders and spinning round on one heel. 'Anything.'

Then she stopped spinning and sat down on the step again. The pair of them were quiet for a moment. It was an awkward silence because neither of them were sure of what to say next. Eddie suddenly became very interested in Butch's collar and bent down to fiddle with it, even though it was perfectly okay as it was.

Suddenly, Flo broke the ice. 'Cute dog.'

'Thanks,' Eddie replied. 'I'm just taking him for a walk.'

'What sort is it?' she asked.

Eddie explained that Butch was a cross between a Chihuahua and a Jack Russell.

'Mmm, feisty as well as pretty,' she said. Butch, who was a pushover when it came to flattery, ran up the steps barking and jumped into her lap.

'His name's Butch,' Eddie told her, 'and I think he likes you.'

'I've just got back from my holiday at Spain,' she said as Butch leapt all over her.

'My holiday *in* Spain.' Eddie automatically corrected her without thinking and instantly regretted it as Flo looked furious.

'Do you speak Dutch?' she demanded.

Eddie shook his head.

'Then shut up. I speak English, Portuguese and Dutch, so it's very rude to correct me.'

Eddie apologised and said her English was really good, which seemed to appease her.

'That's okay,' she replied with a smile, then she stood up and ran down the steps with Butch under her arm. 'It's forgotten. Can I come on your walk with you?'

Flo was the same age as Eddie and lived with her parents in the house next door to Aunt Budge – or in a flat on the top floor, anyway. She had long dark hair and flashing green eyes and was just a little bit taller than Eddie. She was also extremely lively and never stopped talking – in fact, she was as bad as Aunt Budge.

Eddie was envious of her confidence and devil-may-care attitude. Butch had already fallen for her, which was obvious from the way he gazed lovingly up as he trotted alongside.

'You should marry this beautiful signorina. She's boss,' he yapped, using an expression he'd picked up from Stanley. 'I love her.'

Eddie laughed and Flo asked him what he found so funny.

'Is it my accent?' she demanded. 'Are you laughing at me?'

'No, I'm not – honest,' Eddie assured her. 'It was Butch; he made me laugh.'

'Why?' she asked, growing angry. 'He didn't tell a joke or say something funny.'

'Well, he might have,' Eddie said, smiling to himself.

'You know something?' she said, stopping in her tracks and putting her hands on her hips. 'You're stupid, you are. You think I don't know you were laughing at me because I said that dog we passed looked more like a weenie pig when I meant guinea pig.'

'I didn't even notice,' Eddie protested. This girl was very easily offended and certainly hot-headed.

'You did – you laughed! I'm going home and you can go back to England.'

'Well, I'm going to be here for a while, so . . . tough,'

Eddie said, provoking her even more. Flo, at a loss for words, screamed with anger and turned on her heel and stomped off.

'What did you say?' Butch asked.

'Nothing. I was only laughing at what you said,' Eddie replied. 'She's definitely one to avoid – angrier than a wet cat!'

CHAPTER FIFTEEN

When Eddie got back to the house, he went straight up to his room, still feeling a bit annoyed with Flo. Crossing the landing, he passed Aunt Budge's bedroom and heard her talking to someone.

'Really, my dear,' she was saying, 'I don't think this Maggie is the one for you. Smoking is an absolutely filthy habit. So disgusting, not to mention extremely unhealthy, and it looks most unbecoming when this dreadful custom is partaken of in public, particularly when the lady in question is sitting on a windowsill as blatant as you like.'

What? Eddie wondered. Who was this Maggie and what was she doing sitting on a windowsill? Unable to contain his curiosity, he crouched down and peeped through the keyhole.

His aunt wasn't on the phone. From what he could see she seemed to be talking to her dressing table. What was she doing?

Suddenly, he heard a very familiar throaty caw and moved closer to the keyhole to get a better look. Unfortunately, though, he stumbled, falling against the door and pushing it open before ending up sprawled on the floor of his aunt's bedroom.

'Speaking of nasty habits,' she said icily, 'it's most impolite to listen at keyholes.'

Eddie flushed deep red with shame and apologised profusely as he scrambled up off the floor . . . only to be greeted by a large black crow.

'Stanley!' Eddie exclaimed, forgetting for the moment that his aunt was present. 'You made it, then.'

''Ello, Eddie.' Stanley chuckled. 'You certainly know how to make an entrance.'

Aunt Budge got up and closed the door. 'Now then, Eddie,' she said solemnly, tapping her foot, 'I think there's something you need to tell me.'

Eddie didn't know what to say. He stammered and stuttered and his face turned an even deeper red. Poor old Eddie tended to blush a lot, turning various shades ranging from light pink to deep scarlet.

'I'll save you the bother, shall I?' Aunt Budge said, clearing her throat. 'You can communicate with animals, birds and fish, can't you?'

Eddie hung his head in shame – his secret was out. Then something occurred to him. Aunt Budge had been speaking to Stanley . . . which meant that she too could understand animals!

'It sounds like I'm not the only one,' he replied defiantly. 'I heard you talking to Stanley – and I also had my suspicions in the kitchen when you heard Bunty ask me if you had a cat.'

'Covered it up nicely, though, didn't I?' she said with a grin. 'Oh, this is so wonderful!' she exclaimed joyfully, letting out a little squeal and clapping her hands together. 'My dear boy, this is such a revelation! I thought I was the only one in the family who had the gift, but here you are, blessed with the same talents as myself. To think – another Intuitive in the family; oh, what joy,' she sobbed, hugging him tightly and smothering him with kisses.

'What did you say I was?' Eddie asked, struggling to get free of his aunt's bear hug.

'You're an Intuitive, my dear,' she declared, laughing and crying at the same time. 'Which means you possess an extremely rare gift. Are you out of the closet?'

'Out of the closet?' Eddie queried. 'Do you mean, am I gay?'

'No, dear, what I mean is, does anyone else know about your talents yet? And do you know of any other Intuitives?'

Eddie sighed loudly. Sitting down, he told Aunt Budge exactly how he felt about this gift. Instead of being proud of it, on the contrary he was embarrassed, and terrified of his secret ever getting out.

'Well, there you go. You're not on your own any more, matey,' Stanley said affectionately, flying on to Eddie's shoulder. 'Your aunty here has the same gift. Marvellous, ain't it?'

It certainly was. Revealing his secret, finding out that he wasn't the only one in the world who could do what he could – and being able to talk about it – Eddie felt as if a huge weight had been lifted off his shoulders.

'Now, you go downstairs and get something to eat,' Aunt Budge said happily, dabbing her eyes with her handkerchief. 'Stanley will be staying in Amsterdam for a while, so there'll be plenty of time for you two to have a good catch-up.'

As he was leaving the room, Eddie turned to his aunt and asked, 'By the way, who's this Maggie you and Stanley were talking about?'

'Oh, some magpie Stanley's got involved with,' Aunt Budge

replied disapprovingly. 'A dreadful bird, by all accounts, who steals from people's houses and has some filthy habits. I was advising Stanley not to have anything to do with her.'

'Don't worry,' Stanley assured her, 'that bird is history.'

'Glad to hear it,' Aunt Budge said. 'Now, Eddie, Miss Schmidt has cooked you up some very tasty treats, and after that you can speak to your father on FaceTime.'

Eddie almost skipped down the stairs. Aunt Budge was fun, and she could speak to animals. Yes, things were definitely looking up.

CHAPTER SIXTEEN

Miss Schmidt had indeed made some tasty treats, and Eddie sat in the kitchen eating them as she busied herself preparing dinner. She was a big lady with white hair that she wore in a bun tied tightly at the back, and as she peeled potatoes she hummed softly to herself. Eddie thought it might have been a Bavarian folk song but as he listened more closely it turned out to be Lady Gaga's 'Poker Face'.

'I don't really care for children,' she said. 'But I don't mind having you in my kitchen.' This was high praise indeed coming from Miss Schmidt. 'Just remember,' she continued, 'no animals and no strange aunt, either.'

Later on, Aunt Budge called Eddie into her office as she was about to ring his dad on her computer. The office was another huge room with a great marble fireplace. Hanging above it was a large oil painting of a man sitting on a camel in front of a pyramid.

'My late husband on one of his digs in Egypt. I'm afraid the camel was rather uncouth – he kept spitting – but my husband was very fond of him,' Aunt Budge said proudly. 'He's your uncle. I don't mean the camel – I'm speaking of my late husband . . . or was he your great-uncle? I can never work these things out. Anyway, all these books you see,' she said, pointing to the walls that were lined with shelves full of old leather-bound volumes, 'they belonged to him – and, what's more, he'd read every one of them. Twice. I'll leave you alone now so you can talk to your father.'

Within minutes, Eddie was sitting in front of Aunt Budge's computer, chatting to his dad. They talked about everything – how much Dad was enjoying the course and how he liked the people of Middlesbrough as well as his fellow trainees. His room at the B & B was a bit poky but the lady who ran it was nice and she gave him a good breakfast every morning.

Eddie told him about Aunt Budge and the boat and how fabulous Amsterdam was. He didn't tell him about the speaking-to-animals thing, of course.

'So it sounds like you're having a good time, then,' his dad said, laughing. 'What did I tell you? You're looking really healthy too. They must be feeding you well.'

Eddie told him about Miss Schmidt and what a brilliant cook she was.

'All I'm having is a vegan sausage roll and a cheese slice from Greggs for my tea,' his dad said, pretending to cry and making Eddie laugh.

'I miss you, Dad, and I promise I'll bring you some of Miss Schmidt's cooking when I come home,' Eddie said.

'Love you, son. Take care.'

'Love you, Dad. See you soon.'

Eddie slept soundly that night in his attic bedroom. 'Things seem to be working out really well,' he said drowsily to Butch, who was curled up next to him as usual on the big spacious bed. 'Apart from that awful Flo, everything's been trouble-free so far.'

But little did they know that trouble was about to come knocking, bearing an invitation, and her name was . . . Oh, never mind, you'll soon find out.

CHAPTER SEVENTEEN

Aunt Budge was in a bit of a fluster when Eddie joined her for breakfast the next morning.

'Dreadful woman,' she snapped angrily as she stood up from the table, waving what looked like an invitation in her hand. 'I was wondering when she'd come calling, bullying me to attend one of her ghastly events. Well, I won't go. She's an absolute monster.'

'Who?' Eddie asked.

'Of course, I pretended I wasn't in,' Aunt Budge declared, ignoring Eddie. 'Whetstone answered the bell and, when he informed her that I wasn't at home, she stuck her foot in the door and tried to force her way in, saying she'd wait. The nerve of her! And to come calling at this hour of the day! Does she know nothing about etiquette?'

'Who?' Eddie asked again. 'Who forced their way in?'

'Vera van Loon, that's who,' Aunt Budge almost shouted.

'V for Vicious, E for Evil, R for Rotten and A for Ambitious, fiercely ambitious. She's a dreadful social climber, a self-proclaimed socialite famous for her flaming orange hair and not much else, apart from that range of cosmetics she peddles on some shopping channel.'

Aunt Budge went to sit down again, but changed her mind as she warmed to her theme.

'You should see her, plastering make-up on some poor unsuspecting woman's face until she looks like a circus clown,' she said with a loud sniff, pacing the room. 'I mean, I ask you. Orange lipstick? Yellow eyeshadow? Ridiculous, don't you think?'

Eddie didn't know very much about eyeshadow and lipstick but he nodded in agreement nevertheless.

'She lived in Paris for years, you know,' Aunt Budge went on, 'but now that her husband's died she's back. I hear that the Dutch are horrified at what she's done to the beautiful old house that once belonged to her husband's family. The Dutch are very reserved, you know – they don't approve of show-offs, and van Loon is a highly respected name in Holland.'

Exhausted by her rant, Aunt Budge finally slumped into her

chair, fanning her face with the invitation. 'Listen to this,' she said, and read out the letter that had come with it.

'"Sweetheart",' she read, raising her eyebrows at Vera's familiarity, '"I was absolutely thrilled to hear you've returned to Amsterdam after such a long time and settled back into your little house."'

Aunt Budge fumed visibly at hearing her ten-bedroom mansion described as a little house by the likes of Vera and muttered, 'The nerve of her!' again before continuing.

'"I'm throwing a little soirée in aid of the Blue Mountains Rare Birds Society on Monday and I would be thrilled if you would pop in." Pop in? How vulgar,' Aunt Budge remarked tartly.

'"It will be a fabulous evening as I'm exhibiting my priceless new collection of artworks and auctioning some off in aid of those poor little birdies in the Blue Mountains." Well, I'm sure I've never heard of any Blue Mountains Rare Birds Society,' Aunt Budge said suspiciously. '"And, as the event is being held on the ground floor, you needn't worry about having to climb any stairs."'

Aunt Budge hit the roof when she read that bit. 'I might be old,' she roared, 'but, as I climbed Mount Kilimanjaro TWICE, I doubt if I'll find Vera's staircase daunting!'

She continued with the letter. '"Look forward to seeing you very soon. Your old friend Vera." Old friend?' Aunt Budge exclaimed incredulously. 'I barely know the creature. I've only met her once and that was enough. Just listen to this,' she fumed, reading out the last line of the invitation. '"PS I let it slip to the press that you may be coming. Hope you don't mind, darling. V. Kiss."'

Eddie thought Aunt Budge was going to explode.

'I suppose I'll have to go,' she said grudgingly after she'd calmed down, 'now that she's told the press. I don't want to be seen as a meanie for refusing to attend a charity event.'

Aunt Budge sat quietly for a moment, studying the invitation with a frown on her face.

'Dreadful woman,' she concluded. 'Forcing me into this situation.'

'Can I come?' Eddie piped up. 'I'll be company for you.'

'Of course you can,' Aunt Budge replied, 'although I doubt you'll enjoy it. Still, I suppose it's all in a good cause. Now, eat your muesli and then we'll go out.'

CHAPTER EIGHTEEN

After breakfast, Eddie ran up to his bedroom to clean his teeth in the little bathroom that led off it. 'Where's Butch?' he asked Bunty, having just noticed that the dog was missing.

'Dunno. Downstairs?' Bunty could hardly speak because the pouches in her cheeks were crammed full of nuts, expanding them to three times their usual size.

Eddie climbed down the narrow stairs that led from his attic into the big room below. He wandered past some gym equipment that Aunt Budge used every so often to keep fit, but then spotted a door that he hadn't really taken much notice of before, thinking it was just a cupboard. Now it was ajar, with a shaft of sunlight shining through the gap, catching the dust in the air and throwing a pool of light on the floor.

Eddie pushed the door fully open and went to investigate. It led to a roof garden. The houses were so close together that you could have stepped into neighbouring roof gardens and walked among the chimneys; not that anyone did that.

He found Butch out here – in next-door's roof garden – being fussed over . . . by Flo.

'I'm just saying hello to your dog,' she said without looking at Eddie. 'He came over of his own accord. I'm not stealing him.'

'I didn't think you were stealing him,' Eddie replied. 'I told you, he likes you.'

Butch starting barking. To Flo, it was just that – the barking of a yappy little dog – but to Eddie's ears he had plenty to say.

'What's wrong with you, man?' he was demanding angrily. 'She's beautiful and she's a really nice girl. Make friends with her, will you, or I'll bark all day and go down into Miss Schmidt's kitchen and steal food. I might even cock my leg and leave a little puddle. You wouldn't be her blue-eyed boy then, would you? Oh no.'

Eddie wanted to laugh because when Butch kicked off he was very funny, but he resisted the temptation. Instead, he asked Flo, 'How's things?'

Flo simply shrugged her shoulders and carried on playing with Butch.

'You can take him for a walk, if

you like,' Eddie told this infuriating girl. 'He'd love that.'

Butch started yapping and running round in a circle excitedly. 'Yeah, yeah!' he barked. 'Let's go to the park.'

'I think he'd like to go to the park,' Eddie said. 'But only if you want to take him.'

'I'd like that,' Flo said and then, turning to Eddie, she gave him a big smile. 'Thank you.'

'Erm, I don't suppose you'd like to go to a party with me and my aunt, would you?' said Eddie. 'It's on Monday.'

Flo thought for a moment. 'What sort of party?'

'I dunno,' Eddie said, already wondering why he'd asked. 'It's some woman called Vera something.'

'Van Loon?' Flo offered. 'Oh, she's famous. Famous for doing nothing. She was on a reality show where they had to live and work down a mine in Germany for four weeks without coming out once. Imagine that,' she said disapprovingly. 'Wasting a whole month down a disused mine just to get on television. She was chipping away at the walls in just a bikini and a miner's helmet, she's so desperate for publicity.'

'Well, don't come if you don't want to,' Eddie replied hastily. 'I was only asking.'

'Is this a date?' Flo replied, smiling slyly.

'No, n-not at all. It's just that I don't really want to go on my own . . . I'm going with my aunt, but . . . well, you know . . . someone my own age would be cool . . . and I just thought . . . it's just . . .' Eddie burbled.

'OK then, I'll come. Your aunt won't mind, will she?' Flo said.

'Of course she won't. You'll have to come and meet her. We're going out now but why don't you come round for tea later, say about five?' he said.

'I'd love to,' she replied. 'I'll mind Butch and take him for a walk and then I'll see you later. *Ciao.*'

'I'll push his lead through your letterbox,' Eddie said as she walked away. Once again, he found himself blushing for reasons he couldn't explain.

When he went back downstairs, he asked his aunt if he could invite someone to tea.

'Who might that be, then?' she queried.

'Her name's Flo and she lives next door,' he replied, blushing even more. 'I met her yesterday. We had a row but now we're friends again.'

'I'm glad to hear it,' Aunt Budge said. 'One should always try and resolve an argument.'

'Can I bring her to the party on Monday as well?' he asked.

'I mean, actually, I already asked her. Sorry.'

'My, you are keen,' Aunt Budge chuckled with a twinkle in her eye. 'Of course you can bring her, if her parents don't mind. Now, let's go out. There's some places I want to show you.'

CHAPTER NINETEEN

They visited the house of the famous painter Rembrandt. Aunt Budge said his paintings were priceless now but when he died he didn't have a penny to his name.

'Imagine if you had a time machine,' Eddie said. 'You could go all the way back to the sixteen hundreds and buy all of Rembrandt's paintings off him because they probably wouldn't have cost much. Then you could travel back to the present day, sell them for millions and billions and then travel back to Rembrandt's time again and give him a load of money. I'd keep some for my dad, of course.'

'How very entrepreneurial of you,' Aunt Budge remarked. 'But totally impossible, I'm afraid.'

Later on in the afternoon, when they were sitting together in a little café, Aunt Budge turned to Eddie and said, completely out of the blue, 'I did offer to help, you know. After your dear mother's funeral, I offered to assist your father financially, but he refused. He's a very proud man, and a good hard-working one at that. It hurts me to hear that such a talented musician has given up his craft for employment in a supermarket. Not that there's anything wrong with that – it's an admirable job. It's just that I'd like to see him doing something he loves.'

She smiled at Eddie and reaching across the table she squeezed his hand. 'I know he gave up music to look after you but I also know that it reminded him too much of your mother,' she told him gently. 'Come along, then. Let's pay the bill and get home. We've got your lovely Flo coming to tea.'

Flo was a big success. Aunt Budge thought she was not only very pretty but also an 'extremely smart cookie', as she put it. The fish were highly impressed with her as well.

'Look at your two fish hanging over the edge of their tank, blowing bubbles,' Flo said, amazed. 'I've never seen a fish do that before.'

Eddie didn't tell her that the bubbles they were blowing were kisses and that Dan was wolf-whistling.

(The fish also got on really well with Aunt Budge, who would sit by their tank and talk to them. They'd tell her wild tales of pirate life on the Seven Seas and in return she told them that she too was nearly captured by vicious pirates on the South China Sea when she was visiting Turtle Island.

The fish had been very impressed. 'Respect,' they'd both said, high-fiving each other with their fins.)

After Flo had gone home, Aunt Budge was singing her praises. Eddie – possibly because he was a bit jealous – said, 'I know she's cool, but she can be very rude.'

'Actually, she's not being rude, it's just the way the Dutch are,' Aunt Budge explained. 'They believe in coming straight to the point and saying it just how they see it. You'll soon get used to it,' she said, laughing. 'Now, go and talk to your dad. He's FaceTiming you at six thirty.'

CHAPTER TWENTY

That night Eddie couldn't sleep as he had butterflies fluttering around in his stomach. He felt as if he was full of electricity, tingling all over, though he couldn't explain why he felt so excited. He'd had a great day out, he'd made up with Flo, Aunt Budge had bought him a really cool outfit for Vera's party (Eddie had been right: his old suit was too small for him) and he'd spoken to his dad, who'd said he was having an interesting time.

Dad, however, had been far more interested in the change in Eddie, who sounded very enthusiastic about life in Amsterdam. Nothing like the unhappy boy waving goodbye as he was driven away in the magnificent car.

Unable to lie in bed any longer because his toes were twitching and his brain was simply refusing to switch off, Eddie decided to go down to the kitchen to get something to drink.

His attic bedroom was one of the smaller rooms but there was a magical quality to it, and as it was at the back of the house the view from the dormer window was of the rooftops. Aunt Budge had been right to pick this spot for him as it suited him right down to the ground.

'It's not time to get up, is it?' a sleepy Butch complained as Eddie moved his feet from under him and climbed out of bed. 'It's too early,' the dog moaned.

'Shh,' Eddie hushed him. 'Go back to sleep. I'm just going downstairs to get a drink.'

Butch immediately sat up. 'In that case, I'll come with you,' he said, suddenly very alert and chirpy. 'If I protect you from ghosts and bandits, can I have a biscuit?'

'There's no such thing as ghosts and, apart from you, there are no bandits, either,' Eddie said. 'But I suppose you can come with me if you promise not to bark.'

'If I don't bark, can I have a biscuit?' the little dog replied, jumping off the bed.

'Yes, you can have a biscuit,' Eddie agreed. 'But only if you keep quiet.'

As old buildings often do, Aunt Budge's house made lots of noises as it cooled down from the heat of the summer day. Pipes rattled and floorboards creaked and groaned as Eddie and Butch crept along in the dark with only the torch in Eddie's wristwatch casting any light.

The grandfather clock in the hall that had once belonged to

a ship's captain ticked slowly and softly as the pendulum in its case swung back and forth, keeping time.

The back stairs leading to the kitchen were very narrow and they creaked loudly as Eddie tiptoed down them, trying not to wake Miss Schmidt, who slept in a room nearby. Whetstone's room was back there as well and Eddie could hear them both snoring, slightly out of sync with each other.

It was at that moment the grandfather clock chimed, causing Butch to yelp and Eddie to leap out of his skin.

'Shush!' Eddie hissed.

To which Butch replied, 'Shush yourself.'

Once the clock had finished playing its chimes and finally struck two, Eddie stood motionless on the stairs, barely breathing as he listened for any signs of life from Whetstone or Miss Schmidt. Judging by the snoring, they hadn't heard a thing, so Eddie and Butch continued their journey to the kitchen.

Eddie got himself a glass of water straight from the tap – Aunt Budge had said that the tap water in Amsterdam was the cleanest in the world – and then he gave Butch a little dog biscuit as promised.

Taking his water up to the morning room, he sat on the

window seat and looked out over the canal and the deserted streets. It was exciting and a little bit scary to be awake in the dead of night when everyone else was asleep, especially sitting in a huge silent room with the light from the streetlamps casting shadows across the ornately carved ceiling. Even Butch seemed to be affected by the silence and moved closer to Eddie as they both sat and stared out of the window into the dark waters of the canal.

'Look at all the bikes,' Eddie said after a while. 'There's so many of them chained to the railings on the bridge. And look at the lights round the arches of the bridge reflected in the water. It's like a painting.'

Very few lights were on in the windows of the houses opposite and as Eddie sat there he felt like he was the only person in the entire world who was still awake.

Then the *Westerkerk* bells chimed the quarter-hour and Eddie yawned loudly. He suddenly felt sleepy and thought it was probably time to go back to bed.

At that moment, though, a long barge caught his attention as it slipped out from under a bridge and glided silently through the water. It looked like it was carrying cargo – the best part of it was covered in canvas that was strapped down tightly. But at one end some of the canvas had come loose and from underneath appeared what seemed to be a pair of eyes – a pair of very large eyes.

Eddie blinked hard. *What on earth*? he asked himself. Quickly jumping off the window seat, he ran and got Aunt Budge's binoculars from her bureau.

The barge was moving slowly as Eddie rushed to the end window and managed to get a good look at the eyes. He was shocked at what he saw. That was no human face! It was the face of a small orangutan ... and round its neck was a collar with

a chain attached. Eddie stared, open-mouthed in disbelief, and as the barge sailed past he was just in time to see the orangutan look up at him and mouth the word, 'Help!'

The barge vanished from sight, leaving Eddie puzzled and worried by what he'd just witnessed. Did he really just see an orangutan or were his sleepy eyes playing tricks on him? It was no good asking Butch as he was curled up on the window seat, fast asleep.

Eddie paced up and down the room, wide awake now and extremely anxious. If he had just seen an orangutan asking him

for help, then that meant the poor thing was in danger. He wondered if he should go and wake up Aunt Budge right away and tell her what had happened. No, he decided, he'd wait and tell her in the morning. One thing was for sure, though – he'd have to help that orangutan. But how?

His mind troubled, he went back to bed and tried to sleep.

CHAPTER TWENTY-ONE

Early the next morning Eddie rushed downstairs into the morning room where Aunt Budge was sitting at her computer, studying the stock market as she did at this time every day.

'Steady on,' she admonished as he charged in. 'Where's the fire?'

'Sorry, Aunt Budge,' Eddie apologised, slightly out of breath, 'but there's something I've just got to tell you. It's really important.' And the report of what he'd seen in the early hours of that morning came tumbling out.

'Whoa, cowboy,' Aunt Budge said. 'Slow down, for heaven's sake. Now, did I hear you correctly? Did you just say you saw an orangutan and it asked you for help?'

'That's right,' Eddie replied anxiously. 'I wasn't sleepwalking or anything. I saw it on the back of a barge with your binoculars, honestly I did. You do believe me, don't you?'

Aunt Budge sat quietly for a moment, drumming her fingers on the tabletop. 'I most certainly do,' she said eventually. 'I was reading the news online just now about someone breaking into the zoo last night and stealing a young orangutan. How they managed it is a mystery as the animals in the zoo are well cared-for and security is extremely tight. It's well-nigh impossible to break in, so I can only assume it was an inside job.'

Eddie breathed a sigh of relief that his aunt believed him.

'Did the poor creature look distressed?' Aunt Budge asked.

'It looked very upset. It had a big collar and chain round its neck.'

'Disgraceful,' Aunt Budge said angrily. 'How dare they treat a poor defenceless animal like that? I shall ring the police immediately and you can tell them what you saw. Then you must have some breakfast.'

Eddie thought that the police hadn't really believed his story as they hadn't been very helpful – in fact, one of the officers had actually laughed out loud. So he went round to Flo's to tell her all about everything that had happened, although he didn't mention that the orangutan had asked for help or how he'd understood it.

Flo was suitably wide-eyed and shocked when she heard what Eddie had to say.

'We have to rescue that orangutan,' Eddie said after he'd finished his story, 'and quickly.'

'But how?' Flo asked, not unreasonably. 'We don't even know where it is. It's hopeless.'

'We could at least give it a try – it's better than doing nothing,' Eddie said. 'Have you got a map of the city anywhere?'

Flo did, and they sat on the floor for ages, studying her large map of Amsterdam with all its canals and waterways, trying to work out where the barge could possibly have gone.

'I told you it's hopeless,' Flo cried in frustration. 'Where would you hide an orangutan? It could be anywhere. It might even have been taken to the docks and now it's on a ship on the way to another country.'

Eddie had been thinking hard. 'Well, I don't believe you'd hide it in the city,' he reasoned. 'Somebody would be bound to see or hear it. I don't think it's on a ship, either. If you were going to steal an orangutan for the illegal pet trade, then you'd hardly pick Amsterdam. They usually get stolen from rainforests. Maybe it's been hidden somewhere quiet and out of sight, like in the countryside?' he said, shrugging his shoulders.

'I'll tell you what: we'll take Dad's boat out early tomorrow morning and look around,' Flo said.

'Can you drive it?' Eddie wanted to know. 'Because if you can't then—'

Flo stopped him in his tracks. 'Do you ask that because I'm a girl?' she demanded angrily. 'You're being soooo sexist and just so you know, yes, I can drive the boat. Can you?' she fumed.

'I've driven Aunt Budge's, but only for a bit,' he faltered.

'Well, I've been on the canals since I was a baby,' she shot back. 'So I'll take the wheel while you look for anything suspicious. Okay?'

'Aye aye, captain,' Eddie replied, saluting, which managed to make Flo smile.

'Now, go back to your aunty,' Flo said, folding up the map. 'I've got to go shopping with my mother. She wants me to wear a nice dress for Vera van Loon's party. Ugh!'

CHAPTER TWENTY-TWO

$\int$ tanding outside the house that evening, Aunt Budge suggested that they cycle to Vera's, which wasn't far. But, as she was wearing a very elegant, long black evening dress with a huge diamond brooch shaped like a star pinned to her shoulder, Eddie wondered if they should take a taxi or the car.

'Good heavens, whatever for?' Aunt Budge told him after he'd suggested it. 'Whetstone's favourite quiz is on TV tonight so I wouldn't dare ask him to bring the car round. Besides, I can ride in a long dress with perfect ease. I'll simply tuck it into my knickers.'

'What?' Eddie gulped. 'You can't do that.'

Flo just giggled. She had arrived ten minutes before, wearing a dress that Eddie thought she looked really cool in.

'I'm joking, Eddie,' Aunt Budge replied, laughing. 'I can keep my dress at a respectable length and still manage to pedal without disgracing myself. Now, shall we go?'

*

Vera's house was enormous. There were two flights of stairs, one either side, that led up to the large ornate front door. Two burly bouncers in dinner suits stood on guard, making sure that nobody got in unless they were on the guest list. They were brothers and both had closely cropped ginger hair. Their names were OJ and Milo and when they weren't working for Vera they could be found bare-knuckle boxing under the name of the Bouncer Brothers.

Eddie stared up at them as they checked out Aunt Budge's invitation. They looked like giants and he asked Flo why everyone in Amsterdam was so tall.

'It's probably because you're so small,' she replied, giving him a playful shove.

Once inside the house, they found themselves in a long hall with a black marble floor and acid-green lights. The walls were painted blood-red and the overall effect made Aunt Budge shudder.

A woman was standing at the end of the room. She was tall and poker-thin with legs that seemed to go up to her armpits. She was wearing a very short pink dress with a matching jacket that had LOVE THYSELF written on the back of it, picked out in diamanté stones. What really made her stand out, though, was her mane of flaming orange hair, piled high on top of her head, with wild, fiery tendrils tumbling down over her shoulders. She seemed very busy, waving her arms about like a windmill caught in a cyclone, screeching and screaming excitedly and taking selfies as each guest arrived.

'Brace yourselves,' Aunt Budge muttered grimly through clenched teeth. 'You're about to meet Mrs Vera van Loon.'

'My dear, dear Lady Buddleia,' Vera gushed as soon as she'd spotted Aunt Budge, 'welcome to Chez Vera. My modest little abode must seem like a slum compared to all those mansions and palaces of yours back in jolly old England,' she bellowed, her voice growing louder so people could hear. 'Now, do tell me, for I'm simply dying to know – how is your dear Queen? I know how terribly close you two are, almost like sisters, I hear.'

She shouted the bit about the Queen extra loudly to make sure that all the other guests in the ballroom behind her heard that a genuine titled lady who was best pals with the sovereign had arrived.

Aunt Budge had always said that she wasn't the Queen's BFF. She'd met her a few times at charity fundraisers in the garden of the Goring Hotel in London and chatted briefly with her about horses, but that was it. They didn't FaceTime each other or exchange Christmas cards. But that didn't stop Vera embroidering the facts to impress her guests.

Annoyed as Aunt Budge was by the embarrassing greeting, she remembered her manners and greeted this woman rushing down the hall towards them like a steam train with a dignified, 'Mrs van Loon, how lovely to see you and how stunning you look.'

Eddie secretly thought that Aunt Budge didn't mean a word of what she'd just said, but Vera was too far gone with excitement at having such a distinguished guest to notice. Instead, she flung her arms round Aunt Budge as if they were long-lost friends and gave her a bear hug.

'Darling,' she gushed. 'Call me Vera – all my close friends

do. And I shall call you Buddy, since that's what I hope we'll become – best buddies.'

Aunt Budge was clearly horrified at the idea of being called Buddy, but before she could object she found herself being forced to air-kiss Vera, right cheek first, then left cheek and finally the right cheek again in the Dutch fashion.

'Now, you simply must meet my guests,' Vera said, grabbing Aunt Budge's arm in a vice-like grip and attempting to pull her down the hall. 'There's the most divine artist who makes fountains out of toilets. Of course, you can't actually use them the way toilets are intended to be used.' She giggled. 'The force of the water jet on your bare *derrière* might possibly send you crashing through the ceiling!' She cackled loudly, slapping Aunt Budge hard on the shoulder. 'Imagine the shock, darling! No, my dear Buddy, they're purely works of art.'

Aunt Budge gave a miserable little sigh and, switching to her what-can't-be-avoided-must-be-endured voice, said something very posh that sounded like 'high Lulu', which Eddie quickly translated as meaning 'how lovely'.

'Let's have a selfie!' Vera exclaimed and, pulling Aunt Budge close to her, she raised her phone in the air and screamed, 'Smile!'

Aunt Budge managed a sickly little grin but Vera curled back her pneumatic lips, revealing a mouthful of extremely large, unnaturally bright teeth.

'That's wonderful,' Vera said, checking the picture. 'I'm posting it straight to my Instagram. I've over two million followers now,' she boasted. 'It's obvious I'm the most envied girl in town. Now, let's go and socialise.'

'Before I meet your guests, there are some little people I'd like you to meet,' Aunt Budge said firmly, tactfully trying to shake off Vera, who was still clinging to her arm.

'Little people?' Vera said excitedly. 'You mean like dwarves? Performing ones? How divine.'

Aunt Budge tapped her foot as she silently fumed at Vera's display of ignorance, and vowed never to have anything to do with this awful woman again.

'This is my nephew Eddie and his friend Flo,' she said frostily. 'And this, children, is Mrs Vera van Loon.'

Vera slid her enormous glasses down her long nose. Peering over the top of them, she looked Eddie and Flo slowly up and down as if someone had just stood in dog poo and trailed it into the house.

Wide-eyed at the sight of this alarming woman, Eddie held

out his hand. 'Nice to meet you,' he said politely.

Totally ignoring him, Vera continued to stare at them both as if she'd never seen ten-year-olds before. Eventually, she spoke.

'How nice,' she drawled in a tone of voice that didn't mean they were nice at all, in fact quite the opposite. It meant, *Ugh, how disgustingly disappointing. Two horrible brats of no interest to me in the slightest, the little snotballs.*

Flo couldn't help but stare in horror at Vera's shoes, which were bright green and had the highest heels she'd ever encountered.

'Beautiful, aren't they?' Vera almost purred 'I can see the jealous glint in your eye. They're Manola Blancos, the ultimate in exclusivity and hideously expensive, way beyond your measly budget. But who knows?' she added with a sneer. 'If you grow up to be beautiful and interesting like me, then one day you might snaffle yourself a rich man who'll buy you a pair.'

Eddie squeezed Flo's hand supportively – he could see that she was about to explode.

'Now then, darling,' Vera said, rudely dismissing Eddie and Flo and quickly turning to Aunt Budge again as if they didn't exist. 'Let's go into the ballroom. There're so many people who are simply dying to meet you. After all, it's not every day they get to meet English aristocracy, is it?'

Aunt Budge sighed and followed Vera into the party.

CHAPTER TWENTY-THREE

'Find myself a rich man, indeed. What century is she from?' Flo fumed as they watched Vera whisk Aunt Budge off down the hall. 'And what's with the weird hair and those clothes? And did you see her big round glasses? Like an owl.' To emphasise this, she drew two circles round her eyes with her fingers.

'Did you see the jewellery?' Eddie said, laughing. 'Rings on every finger, and that big chunky necklace. Do you think all those emeralds and rubies are real? Even her mobile is covered in jewels.'

'How nice,' Flo said, mimicking Vera, sucking her cheeks in and lowering her eyelids. It made them both laugh, which delighted Eddie as they really seemed to be getting on with each other.

'Look at her,' Eddie said. 'She can hardly walk.'

'Gross,' Flo remarked, watching Vera tottering down the

hall in those ridiculously high heels with poor Aunt Budge in tow. 'Her eyes are like a lizard's and she gives off a bad vibe.'

'Come on, we'd better go after them,' Eddie said. 'Aunt Budge might want rescuing.'

'I'm desperately wanting to see the ballroom,' Flo replied. 'I bet it's gross.'

'You mean you desperately want to see the ballroom,' Eddie corrected her, instantly regretting it for the second time.

Only Flo didn't scowl; she let him get away with it this time. Instead, she smiled. 'Thank you, Mr English Teacher,' she teased, making Eddie feel ashamed. 'Let us both go desperately into the ballroom, then.'

'That's . . .' began Eddie, then thought better of it. Flo was hurrying ahead, anyway.

'Wow,' Flo exclaimed as she looked round the ballroom. 'It's like a crazy art gallery.'

Eddie couldn't help but agree as he stared at a four-metre-high keyhole made out of lime-green plastic that was propped against the wall. Next to it was a ginormous lump of concrete covered in graffiti. Suspended from the ceiling in place of the beautiful chandeliers that had once illuminated the room, were

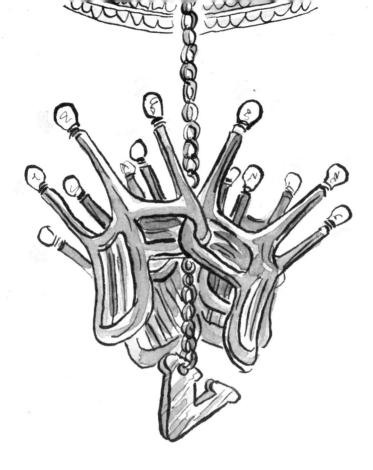

a set of bright-red garden chairs with a light bulb attached to the end of each leg.

This was just a small part of Vera's modern-art collection that she'd 'paid an absolute fortune for, darling', as she never tired of telling anyone who'd listen.

There was an amazing buffet table laden with all manner of weird and exotic food.

'Yuck,' Eddie said in disgust as he stared in disbelief at a pig's head with an apple in its mouth that sat on a huge platter.

'Double yuck,' Flo replied, pointing at a pie that had pigeons' feet and beaks sticking out of the top of the pastry lid.

There was, however, some extremely luscious fruit on display, including a bowl of glistening raspberries that they immediately headed for.

'Mmmm,' Eddie said, helping himself to a big handful. 'Thankfully, there's something normal to eat.'

Flo, munching on a large slice of pineapple, could only nod in agreement.

After they'd stuffed their faces, Flo went off to investigate Vera's 'artworks' and Eddie went in search of Aunt Budge. He found her with Vera and a group of people all staring at a huge canvas that was painted bright orange.

Eddie could hear Vera prattling on as he pushed his way through the crowd.

'Alfredo, who, as you may know, is the up-and-coming Italian artist, followed me halfway round the world to persuade me to sit for him,' she bragged. 'In the end, I had to agree and what you see before you is the result.'

Everybody nodded and said 'ooh' and 'aah', except for Aunt Budge, who just coughed.

'It's my hair,' Vera rattled on proudly, patting her head. 'He said that after studying me he simply couldn't capture the unusual bone structure of my face so he chose to paint my hair instead. Well, it's what I'm famous for, isn't it? My flaming orange locks.' She simpered, tossing her head so her mountain of hair shook. 'It's called *Hair in the Sunrise.* Stunning, isn't it?'

Everyone nodded knowingly as if they understood, and said 'ooh' and 'aah' again, apart from Aunt Budge, who tried to get away but couldn't as Vera still held her arm in a vice-like grip and wasn't letting go for anything.

There was also a magician walking round the room, performing some close-up magic. Eddie stood and watched as he popped a number of ping-pong balls out of his mouth, followed by a length of silk handkerchiefs.

'Do you like magic?' a voice behind him said, and Eddie turned to find a tall man towering over him. Eddie instantly felt uneasy about this character; there was something very sinister about him. As well as being tall and thin, his bony face reminded Eddie of a skull as he peered down disdainfully with cold, hooded eyes from behind a pair of wire spectacles.

'I don't mind it,' Eddie replied. 'Do you?'

'I suppose you could say I am a magician. My name is Dr Lockjaw. I can change people's faces, alter their features entirely. Make their noses smaller, tighten their skin, give them back their youth. Wouldn't you say that makes me a magician?'

'No,' Eddie replied, 'I'd say that makes you a plastic surgeon.'

'Smart, eh?' Dr Lockjaw said, obviously not amused. He seemed to be studying Eddie's face intently, and it made Eddie feel very uncomfortable.

'You see that little red spot on your chin?' Lockjaw said. 'I could zap that off in seconds with my laser.'

Eddie wiped his chin. 'It's not a spot,' he replied indignantly, 'it's a raspberry seed. I've just eaten a load of them off the buffet.'

'You've just reminded me why I dislike children so much. Good evening to you,' Lockjaw snapped, and then vanished into the crowd.

'Weirdo,' Eddie said, watching him go.

Then a woman in a large hat rushed over and asked, 'Who are you? I work on *Utterly Divine, Darling*. It's an arts and fashion mag, very high class – we only cover the best.

So are you anyone interesting that I should know about? Any goss?'

'Sorry, no,' Eddie replied. 'I'm just here with my aunt and my friend.'

'Time-waster,' the woman snapped. Quickly brushing past him in a huff, she ran after a man she'd spotted, shouting, 'Marcus, Marcus, a few words about your latest play? I hear the reviews weren't very kind.'

Eddie thought he'd better go and rescue Aunt Budge, trying his best to avoid the weirder people in the room, which wasn't easy as there seemed to be quite a lot of them about.

CHAPTER TWENTY-FOUR

Having escaped Vera's clutches, Aunt Budge headed for the garden to see what damage the insufferable Mrs van Loon had inflicted out there. She also felt the need to get a bit of fresh air as the room was growing very hot.

Eddie wanted some more of those plump, juicy raspberries from the buffet, so he told Aunt Budge he'd join her later.

On the way, his eye was caught by a small painting hanging on the wall, lit by a bright spotlight. He studied it, unable to make out what it was supposed to be. It just looked like an orange blob with two white dots for eyes.

He felt a hand gripping his shoulder. Without even looking, Eddie immediately knew it was Vera van Loon because of the overpowering, cloying smell of the awful perfume she soaked herself in. It was so strong that it clung to everything and everyone around her.

'You like this painting?' Vera purred like a cat about to

pounce on a mouse. 'It's charming, isn't it? So simple yet so meaningful.'

'What is it?' Eddie asked.

'What do you think it is?' she said, squeezing his shoulder harder. Having Vera's inch-long fingernails so close to his face made Eddie feel extremely uncomfortable.

He thought for a moment. 'An orange with eyes?'

Vera made a noise that she thought of as a girlish laugh, but it actually sounded like someone scraping the bottom of a pan with a knife.

'You poor uneducated orphan of the British slums,' she sneered. 'You are obviously an ignoramus when it comes to art.'

'No, I'm not.' Eddie was quick to defend himself. 'I really like Banksy. He's brilliant, and his street art costs millions to buy. Oh, and by the way,' he added, shaking free of Vera's grip, 'I don't live in a slum and I have a dad.'

'Whatever,' Vera said dismissively. 'Banksy is just a common street cartoonist who scribbles on walls. But this precious work of art,' she said, pointing at the orange blob, 'is totally unique. It's an abstract of an orangutan. Just look at the beautiful colour and texture of that utterly divine coat. Can't you tell, child?'

Eddie tilted his head sideways to study the painting, but it still looked like a blob to him.

'No, sorry,' he admitted. 'I can't see it. What's it worth?'

'It's on sale for a hundred thousand euros,' Vera said proudly, 'and worth every cent.'

Eddie started to laugh. 'You're joking,' he said between giggles. 'A little kid of three could do better than that. Who painted it?'

'Me,' Vera replied coldly.

Eddie stopped laughing immediately. He wasn't sure what to say after putting his foot in it big time like that, so he just gave Vera a sheepish grin and mumbled, 'Sorry.'

Vera stared at him long and hard.

'Let's not keep in touch, eh?' she suggested, giving him a look that could poison a reservoir before flouncing off in a huff, leaving Eddie feeling very embarrassed. Vera van Loon might be awful, but he hadn't meant to offend her.

In the meantime, Flo had been grabbed by three of Vera's so-called beauty technicians, who had forced her into a chair for what they described as 'a complete makeover'. A makeshift beauty studio had been erected in the corner of the room behind a large white screen that had Van Loon Cosmetics written across it in large pink letters.

'Well then, what have we here?' the man said, studying Flo as if she were a specimen under a microscope. 'That long hair will have to go – it's so last year. Perhaps I'll shave it all off except for a little tuft in the front, which I'll dye white, or maybe a shocking pink. Yes, that would look cute, don't you think, girls?'

The two women who were also part of the team nodded their heads in agreement. 'Make-up-wise, I think I'll tattoo some eyebrows on her and maybe pump up those lips a little bit,' one of them said.

'Yes, and lots of black round the eyes and maybe a nose piercing or perhaps a couple in the lips as well,' the other one – who had ridiculously long blue eyelashes – suggested.

'I'm too young for make-up!' Flo protested. 'I'm only ten and I don't want a nose ring, so if you don't let go of me I'm going to have to punch you . . .'

The three technicians stood back. 'Nasty,' the man said.

'Aggressive,' the woman with the blue eyelashes remarked.

'She's not worth the bother,' the other woman said. 'She's too plain, anyway. Send it away.'

Flo jumped quickly out of the chair and ran in the direction of the garden, but she was stopped in her tracks by a man dressed as a circus ringmaster. He was tall, with a black moustache that curled up at the ends, and wore a black-and-purple tailcoat, striped purple trousers and black riding boots that made him look very sinister indeed. There were two sad-faced clowns hovering near him, one of them carrying an accordion while the other had a small drum hanging on a strap round his waist.

'Why the rush, little maid?' the ringmaster exclaimed, taking his top hat off and bowing low. 'Why not visit my circus? The show will begin shortly.'

'What circus?' Flo asked. She was extremely dubious about this man, as well she might be, for his circus didn't make people happy – it scared them and made young children cry.

'Guess what's at the bottom of the garden?' He leered, revealing a mouth full of gold teeth.

'Fairies,' Flo replied.

The ringmaster cackled. 'I'm afraid the goblins ate them, my dear, but I do have a two-headed cobra, vampire bats, wolves, a giant tarantula, a man-eating rat, Medea the mermaid – half woman, half fish! Then there are my clowns . . . they'd just love to meet you.'

He started to sing, the two clown musicians accompanying him, playing a strange, eerie tune on their instruments.

'Oh, I love all my animals,

The cobra and the bat,

The screeching owl, the howling wolf,

The spider and the rat.

My circus is unique, my dears,

I'll awaken all your darkest fears,

So roll up! Roll up! Buy a ticket if you dare,

And pay a little visit to my Circus of Nightmares.'

As he sang, a group of clowns slowly crept out of the shadows of the garden and gathered behind him. But they weren't happy, funny clowns. They were creepy, evil clowns, beckoning Flo to come and join them.

Flo did the sensible thing. She turned quickly and made a run for it. This was the weirdest, not to mention creepiest, party she'd ever been to. Not that she'd been to many parties.

Dodging a woman who was eating fire, she went in search of Eddie, to tell him all about it.

CHAPTER TWENTY-FIVE

Forgetting that he'd told Aunt Budge he would join her in the garden, Eddie decided to explore. He seemed to have lost Flo and was finding the room stuffy and noisy, and Vera's friends either boring, rude or scary.

He'd noticed a series of doors leading off the long hall and, being the curious type, he couldn't resist seeing what was behind them. Opening one and peering round it, Eddie found a dimly lit room, the walls decorated a deep purple and the furniture covered in fake leopard-print fabric, and framed photographs of a grinning Vera accompanied by less famous people on every surface.

'Yuck,' Eddie said, closing the door behind him, and went to investigate the next room. The curtains were drawn and it was pitch-black. He crept cautiously inside and, as he felt along the wall for a light switch, a scratchy voice suddenly spoke out of the darkness.

'What do you want?' it said, making Eddie jump.

'Er . . . sorry,' Eddie replied apologetically. 'I was just having a look around, you see.'

'Take the cover off,' the strange voice demanded.

'Erm, I haven't got a cover on,' Eddie explained nervously. 'I'm wearing my new jacket.'

'Not you! Me,' the voice snapped impatiently. 'Don't be so stupid. Turn the light on and then take the cover off me. The switch is by the door.'

Eddie found the switch and turned the light on, and, once his eyes had become accustomed to the glare, he realised this must be Vera's office. Looking around to see who the voice belonged to, it seemed to him that the room was empty.

'Hello!' Eddie shouted lamely, staying safely by the door in case he had to make a quick exit. 'Hello! Who's there?'

The voice sighed loudly in frustration. 'I'm here, by the far window.'

Eddie still couldn't see anyone, just the thick velvet curtains.

'Are you a ghost?' he asked uncertainly.

'Of course I'm not a ghost,' the voice replied angrily. 'You really are as thick as a ship's deck plank. I told you, I'm right next to the window. Open your eyes.'

Eddie suddenly noticed that there was a dome-shaped lump next to the curtains, covered by the same fabric. The voice was coming from inside it.

Carefully, Eddie pulled off the velvet cover and to his surprise he saw that it was a parrot in a cage.

'About bloomin' time,' the parrot said. 'It was stifling in there.'

CHAPTER TWENTY-SIX

'Um, hi,' said Eddie to the parrot.

'The name's Casey,' the bird said, 'and who are you?'

Eddie was about to tell him, but the parrot interrupted. 'If it's Mr Burglar, then help yourself. You won't hear a peep out of me.' The bird cocked his head to one side and fixed Eddie with a beady eye. 'Take everything, if you like. I couldn't care two hoots cos I hate the old bag and she hates me. If you're looking for the safe, then it's behind that picture of her over the fireplace. I know the combination. So go on – empty it, why don't you?'

'I'm not a burglar, I'm Eddie,' the boy explained, 'and I've come to the party with my aunt and my friend. I was just having a look around. Sorry.'

'No need to apologise to me, pal,' the parrot cackled. 'Help yourself.' Then he stopped talking for a moment as if something had just occurred to him. ''Ere, hang on a mo,' he said. 'You can understand me, can't you?'

'Perfectly,' Eddie replied. 'I can understand every word. I'm an Intuitive, you see.' It was the first time he'd admitted that to anyone other than Aunt Budge, and a little shiver ran down his spine.

'Well, paint me grey and call me a pigeon!' Casey exclaimed, letting out a long, low whistle. 'I'd heard about humans like you but I didn't believe those tales. Thought it was a load of old codswallop. Well,' he said, slightly overwhelmed, 'I never thought I'd meet one of your lot, but tell me what's a nice lad like you doing hanging round Vera van Loon?'

'I'm not,' Eddie replied. 'My aunty was invited and I tagged along. I'd never met Vera before tonight and I can't say I like her.'

'Good instincts. She keeps me locked up in here out of sight because she hates me. The only reason I haven't been dumped in the canal is because I was a gift from the Preservation of Parrots lot and it would make them suspicious if her 'beloved pet', as she calls me, suddenly vamoosed, never to be seen again.'

'Why would they give her a parrot if they knew she didn't like birds?' Eddie asked.

'They think she loves birds,' Casey crowed, hopping from side to side on his perch. 'But she hates 'em. In fact, she hates all animals.'

'But my Aunt Budge said Vera is always holding charity events and fundraising for animals.'

Casey laughed so hard he almost fell off his perch.

'It's all one big scam, kid,' Casey said. 'The money raised is split seventy–thirty and there's no prizes for guessing who takes the bigger part.'

'That's rotten,' Eddie said, frowning. 'Stealing money meant for a charity?'

'I've been telling you, she's rotten to the core . . . and,

what's worse, she's so rich she doesn't even need that charity money. She's just a greedy, heartless thief.' Casey ruffled his feathers with indignation. 'And there's more,' he went on. 'That cosmetics clinic of hers certainly ain't above board and squeaky clean. I know for a fact that she—'

He broke off suddenly as the door creaked open slowly.

'Uh-oh,' Casey said quietly. 'Speak of the devil and she's bound to turn up.'

Only it wasn't Vera, it was Flo.

'I've been looking all over for you, Eddie,' she complained. 'Then I heard your voice from outside. Who are you talking to?'

'The parrot,' Eddie replied airily, nodding towards Casey.

'Oh, how lovely!' Flo exclaimed, rushing over to the cage, making baby noises and speaking in Dutch to Casey.

Casey swore in response. Squawking angrily at Eddie, he said, 'Will you tell Miss Soppy Knickers that I'm nobody's good boy and that I am, in fact, fifty years of age and, if I may say so myself, I've never looked better.'

'Wow, that's amazing,' Eddie said. 'You don't look your age.'

'What's amazing? Speaking Dutch?' a confused Flo asked. 'And, if I don't look ten, then how old do I look?'

'I wasn't talking to you, Flo. I was talking to the . . . erm . . . parrot.' Eddie felt his cheeks flushing.

'Tell her to sling her hook,' Casey squawked. 'This is a boys-only club.'

'Don't be so rude,' Eddie told him, wishing he'd covered the parrot's cage up.

'What have I said that was rude?' Flo looked more than a little puzzled now.

'Not you, Flo, the parrot.' Eddie was growing more panicky by the second.

'You act like you can understand this bird's squawks and the racket it's making,' she said, peering at him quizzically.

'Tell her I don't squawk and make a racket,' Casey said, ruffling up his feathers again indignantly. 'I speak beautifully.'

'She didn't mean to be rude. She just can't hear you, that's all,' Eddie explained, trying to mollify the bird.

'Will someone explain to me what's going on?' Flo demanded, stamping her foot, her face screwed up with anger. 'Are you playing a trick on me, Eddie?'

'You might as well know the truth,' Eddie sighed. Sitting down on the arm of a chair, he began to explain that he could understand and communicate with animals.

Flo's mouth hung open. 'No way,' she said. 'Are you for real?'

'I knew you wouldn't believe me,' Eddie replied, a little annoyed. 'I'm sorry I told you now.'

Casey started squawking.

'What's the parrot saying now, then?' Flo asked. 'Go on, tell me.'

'He says why don't you get a piece of paper and write something down without me seeing, then show it to him and he'll tell me what it says.'

Finding a piece of paper and a pen on Vera's desk, Flo wrote down a short sentence. 'I don't even know why I'm doing this,' she muttered as she scribbled on the paper. 'Because I just don't believe that a parrot can read.'

Casey swore again.

Flo ordered Eddie to close his eyes and turn round, then held the paper up for Casey to see. The bird studied it for a moment before producing what to Flo sounded like a series of screeches.

'Okay, what did I write, then?' Flo asked, folding her arms. 'What did the parrot say?'

'He said you wrote English boys are crazy and he also said your writing is terrible.'

Flo looked totally dumbfounded.

'That's shut her up,' Casey cackled, doing a little dance along his perch. 'Now, listen to what I have to say.'

'It's a trick,' Flo moaned. 'It has to be.'

'Tell her to button her lip,' Casey said. 'What I'm going to tell you is important.'

Eddie asked Flo to keep quiet for a moment as Casey had important news.

Stunned, the girl simply nodded and slumped into an armchair.

'You know what Vera's motto is?' Casey said, lowering his voice. '"Animals are only fit for eating, wearing and experimenting on in the name of beauty." Quite a few animals have gone into that cosmetics research laboratory of hers – and haven't come out again. The more exotic the animal, the better. Only the other day I heard her on that phone of hers talking about an orangutan.'

Eddie put two and two together and quickly came up with the solution.

'So it was her, then!' he shouted, jumping up and down indignantly. 'It was Vera who stole the orangutan. Do you know where it was going?'

Casey had a think, scratching his beak with a claw. 'I bet she's taken him to that laboratory of hers.'

'Where is it?' Eddie implored the bird.

'The lab is somewhere in the *Amstelveen*, in the countryside. I went there once but couldn't see much as my cage was covered up. It looks like an ordinary—'

Before he could finish, the door was flung open . . . and there stood an extremely angry Vera.

CHAPTER TWENTY-SEVEN

'So this is how you repay my hospitality!' she hissed, lurching menacingly towards them. 'By creeping around my house, looking for something to steal, no doubt.'

'We only came in to see the parrot, honestly,' Eddie tried to explain.

'Shurrup,' Vera slurred. 'You've not only insulted my painting but now here you are attempting to rob me.'

'I'm not trying to steal from you!' Eddie exclaimed.

'You can't fool me,' she snarled. 'You came in here to rob me, didn't you? Didn't you!'

She was screaming in rage now, and dangerous with it. Grabbing Eddie by the ear, she dragged him towards her. 'That old fossil you call an aunt should know better than to bring a thieving street orphan into my home, but I'll teach you some manners, you little rat.' She started shaking him.

'Leave him alone!' Flo shouted as she tried to pull Vera off Eddie. 'He wasn't doing anything wrong.'

'Liar!' Vera snarled, and lashed out at Flo, who went flying across the desk, knocking a pile of papers and a lamp to the floor.

'Pick 'em up,' Vera ordered, towering over Flo menacingly, but still holding on tightly to Eddie by his hair now, not his ear. 'Now!' she roared, lurching backwards in her ridiculous heels and crashing into the pedestal on which Casey's cage sat.

Flo's cheeks were burning with anger as she hastily gathered up all the papers and put them back on the desk.

Then the cage, which had been wobbling dangerously, finally lost its balance and fell to the floor noisily. Its door sprang open with the impact, allowing Casey to escape.

'Now then,' Vera hissed, turning her attention back to Eddie and pushing her face close to his, 'I'm going to give you one last chance to tell me what you've stolen before I slap an answer out of you.'

With perfect timing, Casey swooped down on to Vera's head and wrapped his claws round a big fat curl.

'My hair!' she screamed, letting go of Eddie and flapping her hands about in an attempt to shake Casey off. But the

parrot was made of sterner stuff. Ignoring Vera's flailing hands, he calmly grabbed another big clump of hair and started to tug even harder.

Vera was hysterical. 'My hair, oh, my hair!' she screamed again, even louder. 'Do something, you brats!' she yelled as she staggered around, trying to repel the bird's assaults.

At last she managed to catch him by his tail feathers. 'Gotcha!' she said, holding him tightly round the throat.

'Think you can attack me, do you? Well, I've got news for you, birdie. I just might pluck you, stuff you, roast you and eat you. How do you fancy that, eh?'

Picking up the cage, she flung Casey back inside, securely locking the door behind him.

Turning quickly to face Eddie and Flo, Vera then lost her balance. The wires and leads attached to her computer had managed to tangle themselves round her high heels. She fell to the floor, bringing the computer, a printer, all the papers, the lamp (again) and a concrete bust of her own head – for which she'd paid a fortune to have commissioned but which was now minus a nose – crashing down on top of her.

'Get out now while you have the chance!' Casey shouted from his cage on the floor. 'Don't worry about me. I'll be fine.'

'You're coming with us!' Eddie shouted back. But, just as he was about to grab the cage, a rumbling noise that sounded like a cross between an angry bear with toothache and a volcano about to erupt arose from beneath the mound of equipment. Vera was shifting.

'Let's get out of here,' Eddie suggested very wisely, but not before calling out to Casey, 'We'll be back!'

The children tore out of the room and collided with Aunt Budge in the hallway.

'Whoa,' she said. 'What's the rush? I've been looking for you both. Do you know there's the most peculiar circus in the garden? Just awful. I think it's time we left.'

'You can say that again,' Eddie replied, hurrying into the hall. 'Can we please go – now!'

'What on earth's happened? Why the hurry?' Aunt Budge protested as Eddie pushed her out of the front door. Flo wanted to stay so she could tell Vera what she thought of her, but Eddie dragged her out after him. 'Tell her later. Let's just go!' he urged.

Jumping on their bikes, they beat a hasty retreat.

CHAPTER TWENTY-EIGHT

B utch was very excited to see them when they got home. He'd spent the night with Whetstone, who'd taken him for a walk round the block before the pair of them settled down on Whetstone's bed and watched a Clint Eastwood film together.

Flo was still bristling with rage. 'She pushed me over a table!' she exclaimed for the hundredth time. 'She told me to find a rich man when I grow up,' she fumed, looking out of the window, 'and she calls herself a modern woman?'

Bunty, who was sitting on the table, eating a grape, nodded in agreement. 'I bet she's never flown a Spitfire,' she said between mouthfuls, disposing of a pip discreetly behind her paw. 'Her type certainly wouldn't be welcome in the officers' mess.'

'I won't need anyone to support me when I grow up,' Flo said. 'I'm going to be totally independent.'

'Yes, dear, quite right, but that's a long way off yet,' Aunt

Budge told her, slightly distracted because she was listening to Eddie recounting what the parrot had told him.

After she'd heard what he had to say, she remarked, 'Well, we can't exactly go to the police and say a parrot told us what Vera's up to, can we?' Aunt Budge tapped her chin with her finger as she considered the situation. 'She might not even have this orangutan in her lab, wherever that is. There has to be some way we can catch her out.'

'Then there's Casey the parrot,' Eddie said. 'We can't just leave him. If she doesn't cook him, then he'll spend the rest of his life cooped up in that cage and permanently covered. We'll have to kidnap him.'

'Vera will have you arrested for birdnapping,' Aunt Budge reminded him. 'Not a good idea.'

'I like parrots,' Flo said. 'So does my father. I bet he wouldn't mind if I brought him home, because that horrible Vera doesn't care. She only bothers about trivial things like how many followers she's got on her silly Instagram. Who cares?' Flo was still letting off steam. 'She's like a cartoon. No woman I've ever met is like her.'

'She's trapped in another time, my dear,' Aunt Budge said, not unkindly. 'Living in a fantasy world and only interested in three things: fame, money and herself. She must be very lonely.'

'How old is she?' Flo asked. 'She could be anywhere between twenty and a hundred depending on which light you catch her in.'

Aunt Budge replied, 'I don't think there's that much of the original Vera left. She's very fond of plastic surgery.'

'Maybe we could tip the police off anonymously?' Eddie suggested.

'No, that's not a good idea, either. What we need is proof. Cast-iron evidence,' Aunt Budge said, pacing up and down the carpet like a detective in a play. 'I'll sleep on it, but what I don't want is you two getting involved in any way whatsoever. Vera sounds like a dangerous woman when angered.'

'We promise,' Eddie replied, but he had his fingers crossed behind his back.

'Jolly good,' Aunt Budge said. 'Now, we've had enough drama for one night, and I think it's time you went home to your bed, young lady,' she continued to Flo. 'Whetstone will walk you to your door. I'll ring for him.'

'There's no need – I can see myself out,' Flo protested.

'Nonsense,' Aunt Budge replied, slightly shocked. 'In this

house, a lady is always walked to her door. It's the gentlemanly thing to do.'

Flo wondered what century Aunt Budge was living in and was about to protest again but Eddie stopped her.

'It's okay, Aunt Budge,' Eddie said, giving Flo a big wink. 'I'll see Flo to the door.'

'Perfect,' Aunt Budge said, smiling. 'Goodnight, my dear; safe home now.'

Flo, having given up on this argument, simply shrugged her shoulders as Eddie led her out of the room.

'You haven't forgotten that we're meeting tomorrow morning to go and investigate?' he whispered as they walked down the stairs together.

'Of course I haven't,' Flo replied, also in a whisper. 'We'll take my father's boat out late morning. See you tomorrow, then.'

Eddie let her out and watched her walk to her front door. 'G'night,' he said.

'G'night,' she responded, smiling as she closed the door safely behind her.

It was late by the time Vera booted out her last guest and staggered up the stairs.

'What a night,' she cackled to herself as she kicked those shoes off and flopped on to the bed. 'I've raised twenty-five thousand euros for those poor little Blue Mountain birdies,' she said, gleefully stretching her arms out and belching loudly. ''Scuse me,' she continued, tittering like a naughty kid. 'Do you know what's sooo sad?' She was talking to the big satin pillow now. 'Those poor little tweety birds aren't going to see a cent of it. I'm going to keep the lot!' Throwing the pillow high in the air, she screamed with joy.

'Those two kids the old girl dragged along with her seriously need dealing with, though, the little scumbags,' she muttered as she dragged herself off the bed and lurched towards the bathroom. 'But the old girl is worth cultivating. It wouldn't hurt to have a member of the aristocracy as my new BFF.'

Gawping into the bathroom mirror, Vera could see she wasn't a pretty sight. Even with her glasses off, she still looked terrible. She'd lost some of her false eyelashes, and her lipstick was smeared across her face. There was also a fair-sized lump in the middle of her forehead where she'd hit it falling over in the office.

Reaching up into her hair, she started to remove a variety of grips and pins, dropping each one into the basin with a ping.

Then, clutching her hair at each side, she lowered her head and very slowly removed the famous orange locks.

Her fabulous mane was nothing more than a wig. A very near-replica of what her own hair had looked like . . . until she'd allowed a backstreet doctor to inject her scalp with his miraculous 'hair-improving serum' that had actually destroyed her famous curls, turning them thin, lank and a dirty shade of grey. They now hung round her bony shoulders like greasy rats' tails.

Vera groaned as she stared at her reflection in the mirror. Had she not been so vain then she could've had her hair cut into a smart little bob and gone grey gracefully, but that was never going to happen. She was famous for her flaming orange hair – always had been – and without it Vera thought she couldn't go on.

Maybe you're wondering why Vera was such a thoroughly rotten person. Was she born that way? Surely no baby is born mean, selfish and cruel? Perhaps Vera could once have been described as lovely until something awful happened to her along the way? I really don't know. What do you think made her the despicable woman she is today?

I'll tell you what – why don't we have a quick look at Vera's past and find out more about her? Perhaps she was once a lovely person but, then again, perhaps she'd always been horrible.

Let's sift the evidence . . .

CHAPTER TWENTY-NINE

Vera was born in a small Dutch farming village, but she hated animals and refused to help out with milking the cow or collecting the hens' eggs. Instead, she spent most of her time in her bedroom, gazing lovingly at herself in the mirror as she combed her hair.

As soon as she was old enough, she ran away to Paris and became an artist's model. She wasn't what you'd call beautiful but she was tall and thin, and with that mane of orange hair she was certainly striking.

After growing tired of standing on one leg wrapped in a sheet and holding a Grecian urn on her shoulder while a group of students painted her, she found a job in the back row of the Folies-Bergère as a showgirl. When one of the dancers was off sick, they'd desperately needed someone tall to parade around, wearing a huge bejewelled feather backpack. Vera got the job.

It wasn't long before she caught the eye of an extremely

wealthy but very old Dutch businessman. She quickly married him, cold-heartedly believing that he was so ancient it wouldn't be very long before he died, leaving her a very wealthy young widow.

Unfortunately, her new husband took great care of himself and took regular exercise, so he was very fit. To the pitiless Vera's disgust, he lived to the ripe old age of one hundred and five, by which time her youthful looks had long faded. If she were to don her feathers and dance with the Folies now, she'd look like a half-plucked chicken.

Vera still partied the night away and hung out in all the trendy places. But she was growing older and her pleasure-seeking lifestyle meant that she hadn't aged well.

So, to keep up with the young set, she spent a fortune on lotions and potions that claimed to restore her youth and, when these didn't work, she resorted to surgery that didn't make her look any younger, just peculiar.

Vera's hair, in particular, seemed to be losing its lustre, and to her horror she'd even noticed a bit of grey. After hearing about a treatment that restored hair to its former glory, she foolishly decided to visit and pay a fortune to the backstreet doctor and . . . well, you know what happened next.

She saw no one for weeks, remaining in her Paris apartment with the curtains drawn and a turban covering her head until the wig she'd ordered from a specialist wigmaker in London arrived.

While in solitary confinement, she'd had a lot of time to plan her next move. She decided she needed a change, but what? Vera had pots of money and, as well as the Parisian house she was living in now, there was an old house in Amsterdam that she'd never visited, which was, according to her husband, a magnificent mansion.

Maybe it is time to sell up and return to the Netherlands, she thought. The more she considered this idea, the better it sounded.

'Look out, Amsterdam,' she said as she stared at herself in the ornate mirror on the wall with an evil glint in her eye. 'Vera's coming home.'

And so she did – arriving with her entourage and totally redecorating the Amsterdam mansion, much to the shock of the neighbours.

The London wig had proved to be a big success – everyone thought it was her own hair. Having worn it for a few years now, you'd have thought she might have forgotten about all those silly schemes to rejuvenate her faded locks to their original and unique shade of flaming orange but, unfortunately, she hadn't.

It haunted her, and day after day she experimented with all manner of ludicrous potions and lotions, none of which helped at all – in fact, some of them did a lot of damage.

She was considering giving up her quest to find that perfect shade of orange when, one fateful night, she happened to be gawping at a wildlife documentary on TV, while sprawled on her bed, shovelling Turkish delight down her throat.

Usually, this wasn't the type of programme Vera would watch as she loathed animals and couldn't care less what a load of monkeys got up to in some rainforest. The TV remote, however, had vanished under the mountain of cushions on her bed and she couldn't be bothered to look for it, so she hadn't changed the channel.

It was the orangutan that caught her interest. She crawled like a giant spider to the end of the bed to get a better look, her eyes widening.

'What a totally ravishing colour that little ape is! That's the exact shade I've been searching for all this time,' she purred as she stared, transfixed, at the orangutan's beautiful shaggy orange fur.

'That's it!' she screamed, having what's known as a light-bulb moment. 'Dr Lockjaw!'

This doctor had been doing marvellous work extracting stem cells and DNA from all sorts of creatures, Vera reasoned to herself, so why not from one of these monkeys? He could extract the DNA that gave that ape such glorious colouring – and inject it into her. She would get her hair back! She was positively drooling at the thought of it.

'I'll ring Lockjaw right now,' she said to herself, knowing the doctor would still be in his lab even at this late hour, as he was obsessed with his research. 'But first I've got to snare me an orangutan.'

Carefully, she hatched a plan. She knew there were illegal pet traders who sold wild animals that had been taken from their mothers, but she didn't want to wait around for one of these to deliver – not when there were orangutans right here in Amsterdam Zoo ripe for the stealing.

Vera knew some extremely unsavoury characters who lurked in the criminal underworld, so she knew exactly who to call. Within half an hour, a deal had been made. For a very substantial amount of money Vera would be guaranteed a young orangutan, to be stolen from the zoo the very next evening.

Her next call was to Dr Lockjaw to inform him of her plan. Just as she had thought, he was still in the lab.

'Is it possible, doc,' she pleaded, 'to extract something from an orangutan to make my hair the same colour as its fur?'

'Nothing's impossible, my dear,' the doctor reassured her. 'I shall commence my experiments as soon as the ape arrives at the clinic.'

Vera finished the conversation and threw herself back on the bed. 'At last,' she murmured out loud. 'At long last!' Then she started to laugh. If you'd heard it, you might have thought it'd had come from a crazy hyena that was on the loose.

CHAPTER THIRTY

By seven the next morning, Eddie and Flo were sitting on the top step of Aunt Budge's house, discussing the previous night's events.

'Good morning!' Miss Schmidt shouted as she came out of the kitchen door below them. 'What has you two out of bed so early, without any breakfast, no doubt? Come, walk with me – I'm going to the shop for milk.'

They had trouble keeping up with Miss Schmidt because she walked so fast, taking huge strides, but eventually she realised and slowed to a gentler pace that allowed Eddie and Flo to trot alongside.

'How long have you worked for Aunt Budge?' Eddie asked her, slightly out of breath.

'Many years,' she replied solemnly. 'Many crazy years all over the world, cooking for her and her husband, His Lordship, until he sadly passed away.'

'You're a very good cook,' Eddie told her and meant it. 'The best in the world, I'd say.'

Miss Schmidt inclined her head graciously and bestowed a little smile on Eddie to show that she was flattered by the compliment. 'I'm from a little village in the Bavarian Alps,' she told him. 'My father was a baker and my mother was the best pastry chef in the whole of Bavaria. They taught me everything I know about cooking and so, even though I really didn't want to be a cook, I ended up as one.'

'Stop talking about food,' Flo suddenly moaned. 'I'm starving.'

'What did you want to be, then?' Eddie asked Miss Schmidt, suddenly aware he was hungry himself.

'I wanted to be in the movies,' she announced, to Eddie and Flo's surprise. 'Dressed in beautiful costumes and dancing a waltz in a ballroom with a man of noble birth.'

'Did you ever try to get into the movies?' Eddie asked her.

'Well, I did appear in a film in Berlin once, which turned out to be my first and only appearance on the silver screen,' she replied with a hint of regret in her voice. 'I was hired as an extra for the background scenes. The stars were the famous German actress Lena Clodd, and my all-time favourite, that daredevil, swashbuckling hero Wolfgang Schultz.'

She stopped walking for a moment and shook her head as she recalled her past. 'That's when I discovered that the movies aren't all they seem to be.' She started walking again as she continued her story. 'My first day on the film set, the director called me over. "You're just what I'm looking for," he said. Well, I thought this was my big chance . . . but as I'm six feet two inches tall, and the same size as Wolfgang Schultz, he wanted me to be his stunt double. "You mean Mr Schulz, the big all-action hero, doesn't do those death-defying stunts himself?" I asked, astonished. "Of course not," the director replied. "He's far too valuable to risk doing all that dangerous stuff, so he has a stuntman. But the stuntman broke his leg and dislocated his shoulder yesterday and we're in a bit of a pickle, so how about it?"'

'Cool!' Flo gasped. 'Did you do it?'

'Of course,' Miss Schmidt said. 'In one single day, I was thrown through a bar-room window thirty-two times and I jumped from a moving train on to the back of a galloping horse ten times. But it was when I found myself wrestling an alligator in a stinking swamp while Wolfgang Schultz sat on a boat having a manicure . . . that I decided the movies weren't for me. So, instead of waltzing with a man of noble birth, I ended up cooking for one instead – him and his strange wife.'

'Don't you like Aunt Budge, then?' Eddie asked her.

'I like her well enough,' Miss Schmidt answered, 'as long as she keeps out of my kitchen. However, when all's said and done, we have been together a long time now and I've got used to the ridiculous situations I sometimes find myself in. Do you know I once made a *crêpe Suzette* on the back of a hubcap in the middle of a jungle in Borneo?'

Eddie had never heard of a *crêpe Suzette* but it certainly sounded impressive. Just as he was about to ask Miss Schmidt what it was and what they were doing in the jungle, Flo groaned loudly.

'Oh no!' she said, pointing at something just ahead of them. 'There's that hateful Vera's house. I hope we can sneak past without her seeing us.'

'Why?' Miss Schmidt asked. 'Doesn't she like you?'

'She hates us,' Eddie and Flo replied at the same time. Then they told her all about Casey the parrot and how they really wanted to rescue him but Aunt Budge thought Vera would have them arrested.

'In that case, I must rescue the parrot from this terrible woman's clutches. It's the only decent thing to do – and I'd like to see anyone try to arrest me.'

'But we can't just walk in and take it,' Eddie said with a worried look on his face. 'She'd see us.'

'You have to be careful – that woman has a very nasty temper,' Flo warned. 'She hit us!'

'Did she now?' Miss Schmidt replied grimly, pulling her cardigan down firmly round her hips. 'I can't wait to meet her.'

By then the caterers had arrived to collect the rented trestle tables and tablecloths, the trays of dirty glasses and plates and the cases of empty bottles. They were in and out of Vera's front door, so it was easy just to walk straight in – or, in Miss Schmidt's case, march straight in.

'Where is the bird?' she asked Eddie.

'In a room down the hall,' he said, leading her to Vera's office. There was no need for any of them to tiptoe or even lower their voices because the caterers and cleaners were already making a lot of noise. Two men went past carrying the huge plastic keyhole Eddie remembered seeing propped up against a wall at the party.

'What is that?' Miss Schmidt asked the men, who were sweating and puffing under the weight of it.

'Modern art,' one of them told her, mopping his face with a rag. 'Someone paid a fortune for this at the auction last night.'

Miss Schmidt raised her eyebrows. 'Modern rubbish,' she said dismissively. 'Some people must have more money than common sense.'

The office door wasn't locked. Once inside, their eyes took a moment to become accustomed to the gloom as all the curtains were still closed, but then they could see there was no sign of Casey.

'You don't think she's cooked him, do you?' Flo asked anxiously. 'Surely even Vera wouldn't do a terrible thing such as that.'

'I wouldn't put it past her . . . but then he might just be in another room,' Eddie added quickly, trying to reassure her.

At that moment, he heard a muffled squawk.

'Shh!' Eddie said. 'Did you hear that?'

They stood in silence, listening out for any strange noises.

'*Squawk.*'

The noise sounded like it was coming from the direction of a big cupboard. Stepping over the debris from Vera's desk that was still scattered all over the floor, Eddie gingerly opened the cupboard door . . . and there, hidden behind a mountain of coats, was Casey, completely covered up in his cage.

'Wicked to do that to a living creature,' Miss Schmidt said angrily, getting the cage out and placing it on a table.

'Phew, that's better,' Casey squawked after Flo had pulled the cover off. 'It was getting hotter than a sailor's armpit in there.'

'Come,' Miss Schmidt said, picking the cage up. 'Now we have the bird, let us go home. Our work here is done.'

But, just as they walked into the hallway, guess who came staggering down the staircase?

That's right, it was Vera.

CHAPTER THIRTY-ONE

leary-eyed, still half asleep and with a banging headache after the excesses of the night before, Vera descended the stairs. She looked as if she'd just been freshly dug up and was clearly in a mean mood – and more than a little annoyed at all the noise and the coming and goings of the caterers.

'Shut that front door!' she roared. 'There's a shocking draught flying down the hall; do you want me to catch my death of cold?'

'Stay out of sight, children,' Miss Schmidt warned in a low voice. 'Let me handle this creature.' She pushed Eddie and Flo behind her, where they crouched low, hidden from view by a large statue.

Leaning against the wall for support, Vera sort of slid down the remaining stairs, yawning and scratching her head to make sure that her turban wasn't crooked.

'What the . . .?' she spluttered, spotting Miss Schmidt with

Casey. Vera lurched towards her to get a better look – she didn't have her glasses on and wasn't quite sure she could believe what she was seeing.

'What are you doing in my house . . . and where do you think you're taking my parrot?' Vera demanded, pulling her diaphanous dressing gown tightly round to cover herself up and staggering a little in the process. 'I must put a sign on the front door saying riff raff keep out. Unless, of course,' she sneered at Miss Schmidt, 'you're applying for the position of the person who cleans out the gutters.'

'I think you'd be more familiar with the gutter than me, Mrs Whatever-your-name-is,' Miss Schmidt replied, steely-eyed.

Vera's nostrils flared and her already bloodshot eyes turned even redder. 'Mrs Whatever-your-name-is? she shrieked. 'Don't you know who I am?'

'No, I don't know who you are. But I certainly know what you are,' Miss Schmidt replied, making Vera splutter with shock. 'You are someone who is cruel to parrots. So I'm taking this parrot to a place of safety, as there have been numerous complaints about your ill treatment of him.'

Vera tried to speak but had a coughing fit instead, she was so outraged.

'And just who would you be?' Vera hissed angrily after she'd stopped coughing. 'And who are all these people who've supposedly complained? Get out of my house and give me my parrot back! You've absolutely no authority to take it away.'

'Haven't I?' Miss Schmidt replied calmly, looking into her handbag and producing a card. 'I'm from the Protection of Parrots League. Here's my identification,' she informed her, holding the card up. Vera peered at it but was unable to read the wording without her glasses.

'Of course, if you prefer, I could get the police involved,' Miss Schmidt said, popping the card back into her bag. 'It would probably mean a charge of animal cruelty, though. Bad publicity.'

Vera silently seethed with rage. She didn't like to be outdone – and she usually got what she wanted by fair means or foul – but this morning it looked like she was well and truly beaten.

'Take the rotten thing, then,' she spat, 'and go before I physically throw you out!'

'Really?' Miss Schmidt asked, icily calm and rolling up the sleeves of her cardigan to reveal a swallow tattoo on the back of one arm. 'Bring it on, baby, as they say in the movies.'

'Oh, just get out,' Vera replied, backing up the stairs, extremely wary of this woman. She doubted that even Milo and OJ, had they been here, could have dealt with her. Vera herself had no chance on her own.

'Good day,' Miss Schmidt said. Casey loudly squawked something pretty rude about Vera as they walked down the hall.

Vera staggered up the stairs, clinging on to the banister as she hauled herself along, muttering dark threats of revenge.

Only when Vera was safely at the top did Flo and Eddie hurry to join the cook and stride briskly out of the house.

'That was so well handled, Miss Schmidt,' Flo said admiringly when they were back out on the street. 'But what was the card that you showed her?'

'My pass for the trams and buses,' Miss Schmidt replied. 'I just waved it under the silly woman's nose and she believed me. Fancy threatening to remove us physically,' she added, smiling to herself. 'Well, let me tell you: nobody messes with Helga Schmidt and gets away with it. Now, let's go home and get some breakfast.'

Meanwhile, upstairs, Vera muttered angrily to herself. 'That lady will get what's coming to her some day soon,' she growled. 'But first I'd better get myself together and visit that batty old Lady Bud. She's going to be very useful when I decide to hit the high society scene of London.'

CHAPTER THIRTY-TWO

'I didn't expect to wake up to a parrot in my morning room,' Aunt Budge said, staring up at Casey, who was perched on the chandelier. 'Come down, dear, and sit on the table so we can have a little chat.'

Casey dutifully obliged and perched himself on the rim of a cut-glass fruit bowl.

Having forgotten about the idea of going out in Flo's father's boat, Eddie had taken Butch for a walk and Flo had gone straight round to her parents' house in an effort to convince them to let her adopt Casey. Meanwhile, Miss Schmidt had set off on her second attempt to buy milk so she could make a late breakfast after all.

'Blimey,' said Casey to Aunt Budge when he was settled on the bowl. 'Two Intuitives in two days. Well, keelhaul a kipper and call me a seagull, I never thought I'd see this day.'

Casey did a lot of talking while Aunt Budge sat and listened, nodding her head now and then and asking him the occasional question.

The fish were in awe of Casey when they heard him say that he'd once belonged to a sailor and had sailed the Seven Seas. 'Coo, a pirate,' they whispered. 'A real-life pirate sitting on a fruit bowl.'

'Eddie didn't break into Vera's and steal you, did he?' Aunt Budge asked Casey anxiously, after he'd finished speaking.

'Not at all,' the parrot replied. 'They walked in, rescued me from the back of a wardrobe and, after a bit of argy-bargy between Vera and the big lady, old Vera agreed to let me go.'

'What big lady?' Aunt Budge asked, curious to know who this mysterious woman was.

'She works for ya,' Casey explained, picking at an apple in the bowl. 'She had Vera dancing a merry jig, I can tell you, fooling her into believing she was from the parrot protection lot. What was her name now?' he said, scratching his beak. 'Miss . . . Smith – that's it. She sounds German.'

'Miss Schmidt?' Aunt Budge exclaimed. 'What on earth is my cook doing getting involved in all this?'

'Ah . . .' said Eddie, returning with Butch from their walk. 'I can explain.'

'Please do,' said Aunt Budge, but not unkindly. So Eddie told her the whole story.

'She's a tough one, our Miss Schmidt,' Aunt Budge said fondly, after listening to Eddie's explanation, 'but deep down she has a heart of gold.'

Butch had never seen a parrot before and barked at him a lot at first, until Casey hopped on to the carpet and told him to calm down. 'I'm a parrot,' he told him. 'An African grey to be precise, currently homeless having just escaped from an evil woman.'

'Show some respect!' Dan shouted as he hung over the side of the tank. 'He's a pirate king.'

'Yeah,' Jake said, agreeing with his brother. 'He's the real thing.'

'Not really,' Casey told Butch in a low voice so the fish wouldn't hear, 'but I was once in the merchant navy. I sailed all

over the world until I got stranded in Rotterdam after my ship left without me. I ended up in the parrots' home. It wasn't bad, just a bit noisy with all those birds kicking off, but it was a sorry day for Casey when I was handed over to Vera as a gift. They thought she was mad on birds – but she hates us and she's worse than any pirate queen I've ever come across.'

He raised his voice for the 'pirate queen' bit, for the benefit of the fish. They shuddered with excitement on hearing this bit of information, sending little ripples across the surface of the water in their tank.

'Wow,' was all Jake could say, blowing a perfect bubble as he spoke.

Butch thought this parrot was interesting but he decided to keep his distance until his old mate Stanley turned up and Butch could hear the crow's opinion of Casey. Stanley was another bird after all.

'Would you look at me,' Aunt Budge suddenly exclaimed, glancing at her watch. 'I'm still in my dressing gown and I haven't even had breakfast yet. I must go and dress. I'd hate anyone from outside the family to see me in my nightwear. Most inappropriate!' But, as she was leaving, she bumped into Flo coming through the door.

'I do apologise,' Aunt Budge said, quickly rushing past her.

'What's up with her?' Flo asked, puzzled. 'Is she annoyed with us over Casey?'

'No.' Eddie laughed. 'She doesn't mind Casey; she just didn't want you to see her in her nightie. That's all.'

'My father would love us to have Casey,' Flo said happily. 'My mother isn't so keen . . . but they would both like to meet him, so could you tell him to behave when they do?'

'Tell her I'll be as cute as a newborn seahorse,' Casey said. 'I'll charm the pants off them and I won't even say, "Who's a Pretty Boy?" for cash upfront.'

While Aunt Budge was out of the room, the three of them sat down to discuss the exact whereabouts of Vera's lab, with Eddie translating everything Casey said for Flo.

Casey couldn't remember the lab's exact location, as he'd only been once when Vera had taken him on her speedboat – the *Sorceress* – to see if he would be of any use in Dr Lockjaw's experiments. His cage had been covered up, but there was a tiny rip in the fabric through which he was just about able to see out. He realised that he was cruising down the Amstel River because he could hear Vera on her phone talking about it. Then, when the boat stopped, he remembered seeing a white house with some black sheds behind it that looked like a farm. There was some lettering on the side of one of the sheds but he couldn't make out what it said, as he didn't have a clear enough view.

Inside the lab, Dr Lockjaw had taken one look at Casey before dismissing him as a scrawny old bird and telling Vera to get rid. She'd considered drowning him in the river at first, but people would wonder what had happened to the parrot, so she'd had no choice but to take him back home with her. 'Hideous bird,' she'd muttered as they sped off down the Amstel. 'One day I'll wring its neck.'

'I think we should take that boat trip right now, like we said we would,' Flo said when Casey told this story. 'See if we can find this lab.'

'Can't we have breakfast first?' Eddie moaned. 'I'm so hungry I could eat my shoe.'

'But then you'd only have one shoe and would probably be seriously ill in the hospital,' Flo said, frowning.

'It was a joke, Flo,' Eddie explained. 'But I really am starving.'

'Me too,' Flo agreed. 'We'll take the boat out after breakfast.'

'Of course, I'll have to come with you,' Casey said. 'Seeing as how I'm your star witness.'

'Don't forget us,' the fish called out.

'And me,' Butch barked. 'You might need backup if you run into trouble.'

'Seems like we're all going. Let's eat and then I'll go and fetch Bunty,' Eddie said. 'She's in my room and she'd hate to be left out. See you in the kitchen.'

CHAPTER THIRTY-THREE

'There's a lot of traffic on the canals at this time of day,' Flo said, shivering slightly in the late morning breeze as she steered the boat down the canal. 'Which is good – we won't be too obvious.'

Butch was standing on the prow of the boat, like a tiny ship's figurehead. He was obviously enjoying himself, his tail wagging furiously as he took in the sights. Casey was in his element perched portside, the breeze ruffling his feathers. 'Ah, I've missed this,' he croaked happily.

Bunty, sitting on Eddie's shoulder, was less impressed. 'Are you sure that this young lady is qualified to drive a boat?' she fretted. 'And is this vessel seaworthy?'

'Of course,' Eddie reassured her. 'Stop worrying and enjoy the ride.'

'I'm not worrying,' Flo said, slightly surprised, as she turned to look at him. 'Do I look worried?'

'I wasn't talking to you, Flo,' Eddie explained. 'I was . . . erm . . . talking to Bunty.'

'Of course you were.' Flo sighed, shrugging her shoulders. 'Of course you were talking to a hamster. I keep forgetting that it's perfectly natural in your family.'

It didn't take long to leave the city's canals and reach the River Amstel.

'Okay,' Eddie said, reaching for Aunt Budge's binoculars, which he'd brought with him. 'Everyone look out for a white house with black farm buildings behind it.'

Dan and Jake were leaping high out of their tank and then landing back in the water with loud plops, ecstatic to be on board a boat again.

'Your fish can certainly jump high,' said Flo, watching them.

'Higher than a kangaroo!' Dan shouted.

'Higher than one of those airy plane things!' Jake yelled.

'You want to be careful a bird doesn't swoop down and carry you off,' Eddie said, laughing at their antics.

Flo stared at Eddie again, puzzled for a moment, before she spoke. 'Are you serious?' she asked. 'Even an eagle couldn't carry me off.'

For the second time that morning Eddie tried to explain that he hadn't been talking to her.

'Don't tell me,' she said, interrupting him. 'You were talking to the fish.'

'Exactly,' he replied and they both laughed.

They sailed up the Amstel for over an hour. There were plenty of houses along the river. They were big and beautiful . . . but none of them matched the one Casey had described.

'Nah, that's not it; neither's that one. No, that's definitely not it,' he kept repeating until Eddie told the parrot to give it a rest.

Realising that they were both very hungry again, the two children pulled over to the bank and moored the boat. As well as an assortment of apples, bananas and strawberries, Miss Schmidt had packed two large slices of bread covered in chocolate sprinkles in their packed lunch.

'It's called *hagelslag*,' Flo explained as she unwrapped them. 'I often have it for breakfast – we all do. It's typically Dutch.'

'Lucky Dutch,' Eddie replied after taking a big bite of his *hagelslag* and thinking that this was the best breakfast in the world.

Butch, of course, couldn't stop yapping because he wanted a lick of those chocolate sprinkles as well. But, as chocolate is poisonous to dogs, Eddie gave him some dog biscuits instead.

'Thanks for nothing,' Butch moaned, slinking off under the seat to sulk and chew on his biscuit grudgingly.

Once they'd eaten, they decided to head back in the direction of home, scanning the right bank of the river this time, with Eddie at the wheel.

'Just don't hit any houseboats,' Flo warned as she focused the binoculars, 'and go slowly.'

'Excuse me,' Eddie replied haughtily, 'I have had some experience, you know.'

Flo just snorted.

There was still no sign of the house and, just as they were about to give up hope of finding it, Casey suddenly screeched, 'Stop! It's over there, in that clump of trees – a white house with black sheds behind it. That's the place!' he exclaimed excitedly. 'That's Vera van Loon's lab.'

CHAPTER THIRTY-FOUR

E ddie took the binoculars to get a better look. They could see the big white house quite clearly from the river, but it was the buildings behind it that interested Eddie. The row of black sheds could be reached from the river via a small inlet, large enough to accommodate a boat.

There was a high mesh fence surrounding the buildings as well as a gate with a sign that read *Verboden* attached to it.

'Forbidden,' translated Flo.

'That figures,' said Eddie.

There was another sign on the side of one of the buildings. Squinting, Eddie focused the binoculars to get a better look. 'Lockjaw Enterprises,' he eventually read aloud.

'That's it!' Flo shouted in excitement before quickly lowering her voice in case anyone heard. 'When Vera made me pick up all those papers from the floor in her office, I remember the heading on one of the letters was Lockjaw

Enterprises. I bet this is where the orangutan is being kept. Why else would there be so much security?'

'I've met him,' Eddie exclaimed in sudden realisation.

'Who?' Flo asked.

'Dr Lockjaw. He spoke to me at Vera's party. Creepy-looking bloke.'

Flo steered the boat towards the jetty, which also had a *Verboden* sign on it, but, as they weren't intending to stay long, they didn't think it mattered if they parked up. They stepped off the boat then crossed the small road and lurked outside the house, doing their best to appear casual as they looked around to see if they could spot any CCTV cameras. To their surprise, there didn't seem to be any.

'If anyone sees us, they'll just think I'm walking Butch,' muttered Eddie as they strolled down the path at the side of the house and towards the gate, trying not to attract attention.

'Keep your head down,' advised Casey, flying past Eddie's shoulder. 'Vera might be skulking around.'

'How are we going to get in?' Flo asked. 'I think that sign with the lightning fork on it means the gate is electrified.'

'We're just going to take a look first,' Eddie replied. 'Then we'll think of a plan. It's just a shame we can't get in now.'

'Who can't get in where?' a familiar voice cried, and with a flap of his wings Stanley landed on the gate, making Flo jump. 'You wanna see what's inside this place?' the crow asked. 'Well, just leave it to Stanley.'

'What are you doing here?' Eddie asked, delighted to see his old friend. 'How did you find us?'

'Easy,' Stanley replied, cocking his head. 'I followed you. Now then, aren't you going to introduce me to your friend?' he asked, nodding towards Casey.

Eddie did so and the two birds got on so extremely well that he had to tell them to keep the noise down – there was plenty of time for chat later.

'So you can understand this crow as well?' Flo asked, a little dazed.

''Fraid so.' Eddie grinned.

'Okay then, big guy,' Stanley said to Eddie in his most businesslike manner. 'What do you want me to do?'

'Fly over and have a look at those huts,' Eddie said. 'See if you can find anything suspicious in any of them.'

'No probs,' Stanley crowed. 'You wanna come with me?' he asked Casey.

'I'd love to, me old mate,' Casey replied, 'but me wings are

clipped. I've been cooped up in a cage for some time now, so all I can manage these days is the odd flap. I'd never get across to those huts.' 'Say no more,' Stanley said cheerfully. 'No need to explain.' With that, he took off to survey the scene, landing on the roof of one hut and looking around, but there didn't seem to be anything of interest. The next hut was the same – all he could see through the skylight was a load of medical equipment. He was starting to think there was nothing in the least bit suspicious going on here – until he peered through another skylight, this time in the roof of a shed situated behind the other buildings. What he saw shocked him so much that he stepped backwards, flapping his wings, and nearly fell off the roof.

Before long, he had returned to the others, telling them the disturbing news.

'There's lots of animals in there,' he explained, 'and all of them in cages.'

'But did you see an orangutan?' Eddie asked hopefully.

Stanley pulled at a few feathers on his chest to straighten them out before replying. 'Yes, I did, and he was sitting in a cage whimpering, poor thing.'

'I knew it!' Casey cried triumphantly. 'I knew this was the perfect place to stash a stolen orangutan.'

'But what does she want an orangutan for in the first place?' Eddie asked. 'It's a mystery.'

'And mysteries need to be solved,' Stanley responded with a wink.

'We'll have to come back much later tonight when there's nobody about and see if we can get in and rescue him. Are you up for it, Flo?' Eddie asked.

'I certainly am,' she replied.

And so, wondering all the while just how they were going to get into the lab, they returned to the boat and set off for home.

CHAPTER THIRTY-FIVE

Just as Eddie, Flo and the animals were cruising down the Amstel, Aunt Budge received a visitor. She wasn't very happy about this because she didn't approve of visitors before two p.m. As far as Aunt Budge was concerned, it wasn't the done thing in polite society, and a visitor such as Vera really wasn't welcome at any time of the day.

'Darling!' Vera van Loon screeched, sweeping into the room like a hurricane, having rudely pushed her way past Whetstone at the front door. 'How divine to catch you at home. I just had to pop in as I didn't get to say goodnight before you left my party. Did you enjoy yourself?'

'Ah yes, the party. I'd like to talk to you about that,' Aunt Budge replied coldly, as Vera air-kissed her before plonking herself down, uninvited, on the antique sofa, flinging her enormous coat over the arm. 'Do make yourself at home,' Aunt Budge said pointedly. 'As I said, I'd like a word abou—'

but before she could finish what she was saying, Vera rudely interrupted.

'What a charming room,' she announced, looking around and scowling. 'So quaint and old-fashioned – and with that look of faded grandeur that you members of the British aristocracy seem to go for.' She gave a little giggle. 'Now, if it were me, I'd knock that wall down, rip out that ghastly old fireplace and paint the whole house black and red.'

Aunt Budge looked horrified, but Vera prattled on, oblivious to the fact that Aunt Budge's face was turning scarlet and she was tapping her foot – always a good indication that she was about to explode.

'Sweetheart,' said Vera, 'if you ever decide to get rid of all this musty old stuff and do the place up, then don't hesitate to call me. My reputation as an interior designer is the talk of Europe.'

'I can quite believe it,' Aunt Budge replied frostily, 'especially after seeing what you've done to your house.'

'Oh, thank you,' Vera gushed, not realising Aunt Budge was being sarcastic. 'People have told me that they've never seen anything like it. One art critic was so overwhelmed by it all he actually fainted!'

'I'm not surprised,' Aunt Budge remarked, giving her a withering look. Then just when Vera least expected it she turned on her, giving her a proper roasting over the way she'd treated Eddie and Flo. 'Perhaps it was all a misunderstanding,' she concluded icily, 'but Eddie is not a liar, and he was rather upset when he came home.'

Vera tried to raise her eyebrows to show that she was surprised, but failed miserably. 'Sweetie, they were in my office,' she protested. 'Probably looking for something to steal.'

'Don't judge my nephew and his friend by your own standards, Mrs van Loon,' Aunt Budge replied grimly.

'Sweetheart, let's not fight over such a silly misunderstanding,' Vera said quickly, before Aunt Budge could kick off again. 'Such dear, dear friends that we are.'

Aunt Budge snorted in disgust.

'I've brought you a gift; call it a peace offering,' Vera continued, handing over a bag tied up with a gaudy pink bow. 'It's a few samples from my own beauty range, made here in Amsterdam in my own laboratories. There's a wonderful wrinkle cream you could do with. I'm sure you'll find it beneficial.'

Aunt Budge wanted to physically grab hold of this awful

woman and chuck her out of the window into the canal. She kept calm, however, and pretended to be interested in this gift so she could find out more about Vera's lab.

'Of course, I assume you only use natural ingredients?' Aunt Budge asked casually. 'There's no testing on animals, I hope.'

'Darling, my products are so pure you could use them on a newborn baby,' Vera lied. 'Everything is completely organic.' Then she glanced at her watch and let out a loud screech. 'Is that the time? I'm going to have to dash off. It's non-stop, busy, busy, busy. Everybody wants a piece of me,' she said coyly.

At that point, Vera realised that she couldn't make as hasty an exit as she'd hoped because of her voluminous coat. Aunt Budge's antique sofa was a big, squashy, elaborate affair. It had belonged to the same sea captain who'd owned the big clock in the hall. It was held together by an arrangement of ropes, and the arms as well as the back were adorned with carvings of crabs, anchors, tiny mermaids and all things nautical. Vera's huge emerald-green coat happened to be covered in a series of little woollen loops, and a number of these had attached themselves to the gilt mermaids' tails.

'My coat!' Vera panicked, tugging to try and free it. 'It's an original Lorenzo de Cazzio,' she moaned as it refused to move.

'Mind my sofa!' Aunt Budge called out, slightly alarmed. 'It's very precious, so kindly go easy on it.'

Vera gave one final tug and, to her horror, heard a terrible tearing sound.

'I hope that was your wretched sofa and not my coat,' Vera said rudely, not bothered if Aunt Budge heard her or not. Flinging the garment over her shoulder, she swept out of the room. 'Cheerio, darrrrrling,' she called out, rolling her Rs for effect. 'Let's do lunch soon.'

CHAPTER THIRTY-SIX

B y the time Eddie and Flo got home, Vera had already left in her high-powered speedboat, heading towards the laboratory. Aunt Budge didn't seem to be around, but she'd left Eddie a note explaining her absence. Having to face Vera van Loon in the middle of breakfast had been bad for her nerves, she said, so she'd gone upstairs for a calming yoga session.

'What are we going to do?' Eddie asked, pacing up and down the room. 'We can't just leave the orangutan and all those other animals in that terrible place. We have to rescue them somehow.'

'But how?' Flo asked, picking up a bottle of Canal No. 9, one of the heady aromas from Vera's Amsterdam range that she had given to Aunt Budge. She squirted some into the air and took a sniff. 'Phew!' she exclaimed, wrinkling up her nose. 'It smells like cat wee.'

Butch was digging furiously at the sofa cushions and making peculiar grunting noises.

'Butch, stop that,' Eddie said. 'Leave the sofa alone. You're always worrying it.'

'I think we should call the police,' Flo said at last. 'Shall I ring them?'

'You think the police are going to listen to a ten-year-old girl?' Eddie asked. 'Aunt Budge said she'd heard on the radio that the police have received loads of prank calls from people claiming they had the orangutan. They'll think you're just another one.'

Meanwhile, Butch had dug so far down the back of the sofa all you could see of him were his back legs and tail, which was wagging furiously.

'Butch!' Eddie shouted at the dog again. 'Will you stop that? What are you looking for?'

'These,' Butch replied through his teeth as they pulled out a bunch of keys that had buried themselves behind the sofa cushions as things so often do.

At first Eddie thought they probably belonged to Aunt

Budge, but, when he noticed that the key ring bore a large gold letter 'V', he immediately knew who their owner was.

'Look, Flo,' he gasped. 'How lucky are we? These must be Vera van Loon's keys! Aunt Budge said she'd been here – she must have dropped them. And look at this,' he added triumphantly, holding up a grey plastic fob attached to the key ring. 'It's one of those things that opens garage doors . . . or maybe iron gates.'

'You think that will open the gate of the lab?' Flo asked excitedly.

'Well, there's only one way to find out, isn't there?' Eddie grinned. 'We'll go back tonight after dark when, hopefully, nobody's there and see if we can get in.'

'What about your aunt?' Flo asked with a worried expression on her face. 'You promised her we wouldn't get involved.'

'I hate lying to Aunt Budge,' Eddie replied guiltily, 'but we can't just sit here and wait for someone to help. Anyway,' he added with a sly grin, 'I had my fingers crossed when I said it, so it wasn't really a proper promise, was it?'

'I give up,' Flo said, shaking her head. 'Tonight it is, then.'

*

Meanwhile, Vera wasn't the happiest person in Holland since she'd discovered, on arrival at the lab, that she didn't have her keys and now couldn't get in.

'I'm sure I had them when I left the house,' she muttered angrily to herself, after she'd tied her boat to the jetty. But they weren't in her handbag and, checking her pockets, she suddenly realised what that tearing sound had been when she'd tugged the coat away from where it had been caught on the sofa. Vera had assumed she'd ripped one of the cushions, but she hadn't – it had been the pocket of her loopy coat.

'They must've fallen out somewhere in that junk shop the silly woman calls a morning room,' she told herself. 'I'd better put my nice, friendly voice on and ring the old bat.'

Aunt Budge had an antique telephone in her morning room and, even though it was old, it was still in perfect working order. When it rang, Eddie and Flo didn't have a clue where the ringing was coming from. Eventually, they realised it came from this strange black object, but they weren't quite sure what to do.

'What is it?' Flo asked.

'It's a phone,' Eddie told her. 'I've seen one in a museum. I think you lift that black handle up and talk into it.' Eddie did just that, but nearly dropped it when he heard Vera's voice blaring out of the earpiece.

'Sweetie pie,' Vera gushed, without even bothering to say hello. 'I've done the most silly thing and gone and mislaid my keys. They can only be in your delightful little morning room. Could you check around that sofa for me?'

'I couldn't, actually,' Eddie replied in a high-pitched voice, trying to sound like his aunt and also trying very hard not to laugh at the same time. 'I'm afraid the hamster ate them.'

'What!?' Vera roared. 'How can a hamster eat a bunch of keys? I've never heard . . . hang on a minute,' she said, realising something wasn't quite right. 'This isn't Lady Buddleia, is it? You're that brat, aren't you?'

'Yes, it is the brat,' Eddie told her in his own voice, 'and, if you want your keys, you'll have to come round tomorrow night as it's not convenient at the moment.'

While this was going on, Flo was rolling about on the floor with a cushion in her mouth, trying to muffle her giggles.

'You see,' he continued, 'we're all going out for the night and won't be back until tomorrow, so, if you don't mind, you'll just have to wait.' And, with that, he put the phone down.

'If we've got her keys, that means she can't get into her lab,' Eddie said. 'But we can . . . and we've got till tomorrow night to do so.'

'Cool,' Flo said. 'Let's rescue that orangutan.'

CHAPTER THIRTY-SEVEN

Vera's screams of frustration could be heard all the way down the Amstel, but eventually she calmed down from a raging boil to a low simmer. Climbing out of the boat, she stomped down the path towards the black sheds. Ringing the intercom on the gate, and having to wait some time before anyone answered, did nothing to improve her mood.

'Answer the intercom, you fools,' she screeched, jabbing her finger repeatedly on the buzzer, 'or I'll sack the lot of you!'

Eventually, the timid little voice of a junior lab assistant answered. 'Is that you, Mrs van Loon?'

'No, it's Queen Maxima,' Vera replied in sweet but deadly tones. 'I thought I'd drop in since I happened to be passing.'

There was a loud gasp, then silence from the intercom for a while until the voice spoke again, trembling now.

'Oh, Your Majesty . . . we weren't expecting a royal visit,' the voice spluttered. 'We're not prepared . . . we haven't . . . you see—'

Vera exploded. 'It's me, you pea-brained nitwit! I've mislaid my keys. Look into the camera,' she hissed, shoving her face into the lens.

The voice gave a little squeal and the gate mechanism activated.

'I haven't mislaid them,' she fumed to herself as the large metal gate slowly slid open. 'I know exactly where they are – that brat has them and I bet he's up to something. If he is, he'll regret it. I'll skin him and his know-it-all girlfriend alive.'

CHAPTER THIRTY-EIGHT

The voice on the intercom had belonged to a young Indonesian assistant called Miss Lubis.

'What are you doing answering the gate?' Vera demanded. 'What happened to the security guards?'

'They're all off with the flu,' Miss Lubis explained, trying to keep up with Vera as she marched down the corridor. 'Dr Lockjaw thought it best that they stayed away in case they passed anything on to the animals, especially the orangutan, as they're very susceptible to human diseases.'

'Boring,' Vera snapped irritably. 'So the monkey catches a cold? Big deal. Where is the doctor? I want to see how the experiments are going.'

Dr Silas Lockjaw had once been well respected, but his illegal and unethical experiments had seen him struck off by the Board of Medical Governors. Nevertheless, he still considered himself to be a genius who could turn back time and make those who were able to pay enough money young and beautiful again.

Vera thought he was a genius as well, which was why she was shelling out a small fortune. She was convinced he'd be able to discover a formula that could turn her hair back to its fiery orange again. The doctor had mentioned something very promising last night at the party and it sounded like he might have found a solution.

'My dear Mrs van Loon,' Dr Lockjaw greeted her, 'you've arrived just in time.'

'Is it ready?' Vera cried greedily. 'My magic serum – is it ready, doctor? Please, please tell me it is, or I'll just positively curl up and die in a ditch.'

Lockjaw laughed.

'Patience, my dear,' he told her. 'The serum is nearly ready. I just have to make some minor adjustments and then you can have it.'

And so it was arranged that, after the doctor had implemented a few swift tweaks, Vera would be given an injection and then put on a drip that would feed a weird liquid into her.

'I've taken blood, stem cells and DNA from the orangutan,'

the doctor explained. 'Once you've had the treatment, however, I'm afraid you'll have to stay in the clinic overnight so I can monitor you.'

Vera didn't care if she had to sleep on the roof in a snowstorm – all she was concerned about was getting the hair-restoring serum. As impatient as she was, she didn't even mind waiting while the doctor went back into his room to carry out the 'minor adjustments'.

One entire wall of the lab was covered in cages containing a variety of animals. There were mice, a rabbit with a bandage over one eye, some doves, and sitting in the end cage, very quiet and obviously very scared, was the young orangutan.

Vera slunk over to his cage and poked a bony finger through the bars. The orangutan thought about biting it hard but she looked so strange, he thought she might be poisonous, so he didn't bother.

'Thanks to you, my little ginger monkey,' she purred, 'tomorrow morning I'm going to have my beautiful orange hair back.'

The orangutan wasn't very keen on being called a monkey, and, as he'd decided not to bite her, he felt that he really had to do something else to show this woman what he thought. He flung a lump of poo at her and then leapt at the bars of the cage, making a lot of noise.

Vera screamed loudly. Retreating hastily from the cage in fright, she skidded on the poo and fell flat on her back.

The orangutan clapped his hands with glee. Jumping up and down, he let out a series of high-pitched screeches, which is how an orangutan laughs.

Vera was livid. 'You disgusting little ape,' she hissed, shaking the messy shoe off her foot and picking herself up from the floor. 'I'd finish you off here and now myself, only I'm going to need you. You see, little monkey, I'm going to insist the doctor makes more serum, just in case I ever need a top-up . . . which means you'll never, ever leave that cage.'

The little orangutan quickly moved to the back of his cage and sat quietly, scared even to look at Vera. As she approached him again, he felt her shadow creeping closer until it gradually covered him completely. He couldn't see the light behind her any more, just Vera's dark shape and her eyes, which glowed yellow like a snake's in the shadow.

'If I were you, little monkey, I'd cultivate some manners,' she threatened. 'Or next time it'll be the cattle prod. A few electric shocks might teach you to behave.'

Picking up her poo-covered footwear between two fingers, she tossed the shoe into a sink for Miss Lubis to clean up. After all, if Miss Lubis didn't do every single thing she was told, whether she liked it or not, then Vera wouldn't give the woman her passport back. This meant that, just like the orangutan, Miss Lubis was trapped.

Realising that wearing a single shoe made her walk as if she had one foot on the pavement and the other in the gutter, Vera kicked it off. The shoe hit a cage full of doves, sending them flapping wildly about in panic.

Dr Lockjaw appeared at the door. 'Before I add the final touch to the serum, there's something very interesting I'd like you to see,' he said, beckoning her over to the security office. The doctor lived in fear of a police raid and, even though there were guards, he was constantly monitoring the security cameras. After all, he was wanted by the police in Switzerland and, if he was discovered experimenting on a stolen orangutan, that would land him back in prison.

Vera mooched, flat-footed, into the office like a sulky, overgrown teenager. She wanted her serum and she wanted it now. She hadn't come here to look at security cameras.

'What is it?' she asked impatiently.

'Give me a moment,' said Dr Lockjaw, fiddling with some controls. 'Just bringing it up.'

There was a row of television screens on the wall so, while he pressed buttons, Vera sat watching what was going on outside. Nothing was happening in the yard so she switched to the CCTV that covered the gate and sat staring at that for a while until, yawning with boredom, she flicked over to the camera that was hidden in a bird box at the front of the house. This one covered the jetty, the footpath and the river. That was why Eddie and Flo had thought there were no security cameras – they were too well hidden.

Vera watched as a couple walked past with their dog. As the camera also had a microphone, she could hear them discussing the price of paint and whether it was worth decorating the spare room.

'Paint it black, you cretins,' Vera said, even though the couple couldn't hear her. 'It's the ultimate in chic. Now, come on,' she snapped, turning to the doctor. 'What is it you want to show me that's so interesting? It had better be good . . .'

Ignoring her complaints, the doctor had rewound a tape on one of the monitors, stopping at a certain point, and advised her to study the film carefully. Vera's voice trailed off as she saw a boat containing two young people she recognised.

'Ugh,' she spat, 'it's those two brats again. What are they doing creeping around here?'

'Keep watching,' the doctor instructed. 'It gets worse.'

CHAPTER THIRTY-NINE

era watched closely as Eddie and Flo's boat sat there in
the water. She wondered what they were talking about
and why they were pointing at the house.

'He's got binoculars,' Vera gasped, 'and he's looking directly
at the lab, the vile little thing. He's even got my parrot on his
shoulder! I knew that woman from the Parrots' Protection
League was a phoney,' she snarled, referring to Miss Schmidt.
'Now they're approaching the jetty . . . and they've got the
absolute cheek to moor their boat!'

Vera's voice rose higher and higher as she watched Eddie
and Flo get out of the boat and stand outside the house. Now,
she could not only see them but also hear what they were
saying.

'I knew they were up to something!' Vera cried, banging her
fist on the desk. 'And now I'm going to find out what.'

A large black crow suddenly appeared in the picture,

perching on the gate. She couldn't quite believe her eyes as she watched Eddie talking to it as if it understood him. It looked to Vera like they were having a proper conversation.

'Fly over and have a look at those huts,' she heard Eddie say. 'See if you can find anything suspicious in any of them.'

Vera turned pale. 'So they're on to me,' she groaned. 'How they found out is beyond me. Someone must've talked!'

The doctor switched to the other camera, the one that covered the glass skylight in the roof. Vera watched in horror as Stanley hopped about, peering down into the lab before flying swiftly away. Then her jaw hit the desk when she saw the bird fly back to the gate and somehow, via a series of long caws, convey to Eddie what he'd just witnessed.

The blood completely drained from her face when she heard Eddie say, 'But what does she want an orangutan for in the first place? It's a mystery . . . We'll have to come back much later tonight when there's nobody about and see if we can get in and rescue him. Are you up for it, Flo?'

'The boy could understand every croak and caw that came out of that bird's beak,' Vera exclaimed to the doctor, incredulous. 'But how? Has he trained it or something? I can't quite believe what I've just seen.'

'Indeed,' said Dr Lockjaw. 'Hence my concern.'

Vera sat, stunned, unable to take it in, all thoughts of her serum forgotten for the time being. 'A talking crow?' she kept saying. 'The brat can understand it . . . and now they know I've got the orangutan . . . and they're going to come back tonight to rescue it? Or so the little fools think.'

'Exactly,' the doctor agreed. 'Luckily, there is no way they will be able to get into the lab—'

Vera let out a scream. 'The keys!' she howled. 'They've got my keys, so they'll just be able to stroll in. They could sneak in and take photos and pass them on to the cops. I wouldn't be surprised if that crow could work a camera, the way it behaves!'

'Calm down, Mrs van Loon,' the doctor said. 'Let me think.' He paused. 'There is only one solution. If they do come, we'll be here waiting for them.'

'Then what?' Vera demanded, not quite convinced.

The doctor gave her a steely grin. 'The boy is interesting,' he said ominously. 'I'd like to find out just how he understood that crow. The part of the brain that governs communication would definitely be worth investigating. A dangerous operation, but then we're not really concerned about the boy's welfare, are we, Mrs van Loon?'

Vera couldn't care less what happened to Eddie. 'What about the girl?' she asked.

The doctor rubbed his hands together.

'All that youthful blood, not to mention the stem cells from such a healthy young specimen? Why, I could invigorate you, rejuvenate you. You'll leave this clinic a new woman.'

'So we just let them come, then,' she said, licking her lips, 'because Aunty Vera will be waiting with a couple of thugs to greet them.'

CHAPTER FORTY

Vera made a quick call to Milo and OJ, the bouncers from her party, barking instructions down the phone and arranging for the two thugs to come round to the clinic later on.

'I have a feeling tonight's going to be my night,' she said cheerily as she made her way to the private quarters that had been done out just like a very expensive hotel room for such occasions. 'I'll have my beautiful hair back and I'll get to silence those two brats at the same time. Perfect!'

She called out to the doctor to see if he was ready yet. He obviously was as he appeared, wielding a very large syringe containing a luminous liquid. Vera let out a squeal of delight.

'I'm going to give you two injections,' Dr Lockjaw explained as she lay on the bed, 'and then I'm going to attach you to a drip. When the two solutions combine in your bloodstream, the pigmentation and texture of your hair will gradually begin to change.'

'Wonderful.' Vera sighed happily. 'Now, let's get on with it, doc.'

At two in the morning, Eddie and Flo crept out of their respective homes without waking anybody and set off on their bikes to Vera's lab, along with Butch and Bunty. The fish had demanded to come too, but Eddie had told them it just wasn't practical.

Casey hadn't been very keen, also for practical reasons. 'I find it hard to keep quiet,' he'd explained. 'I have spontaneous outbursts that I just can't control. I don't want to give you away, so, if you don't mind, I'll stay here and hold the fort.'

The streets were quiet with virtually no traffic, just a few cyclists on their way home from the restaurants and bars where they worked. The road that ran along the river towards the lab was dark, with hardly any lights on in the houseboats and houses. It seemed to Eddie that the whole of Amsterdam was sleeping except for him, Flo, Butch and Bunty.

They parked the bikes in a bush and tiptoed down the path towards the gate.

'I still reckon the plastic fob on Vera's key ring opens the gate,' Eddie whispered to Flo. 'I think that's a sensor on the intercom.'

'Try it, then,' Flo urged. 'See if it works.'

It did work. The gate slid silently open, allowing Eddie and Flo and the animals to creep in and make for the hut where Stanley had seen the orangutan.

'I wonder which one opens the door?' Eddie mused, looking at the jumble of keys in his hand.

'Try the fob again,' Flo suggested. 'There's another sensor on the side there.'

The fob did indeed open the door, and soundlessly the gang entered the lab. Apart from a blue working light, the place was in virtual darkness.

'Look at all these cages,' Bunty whispered, peering over the edge of Eddie's jacket pocket. 'And look at all the poor animals locked up inside. It's criminal!' she added. 'Plain criminal.'

'Don't worry, we'll set them all free,' Eddie reassured her, 'but first let's find the orangutan.'

It was Butch who found him. Thanks to the dog's keen sense of smell, he immediately sniffed out the orangutan's cage and pitter-pattered across the floor towards it.

Eddie and Flo followed him, creeping noiselessly across

the lab. Kneeling down in front of the cage, Eddie spoke to the imprisoned creature.

'Hi,' he said softly. 'I'm Eddie. Do you remember me? You saw me in the window when you were on the boat.'

The little orangutan crawled towards Eddie. Reaching out through the bars of the cage, he gave Eddie's finger a little squeeze.

'Are you going to take me back to my mother?' the orangutan asked, his big dark eyes shining in the blue light. 'I don't like it here. Those bad people hurt me.'

'I'm going to get you out of here if it's the last thing I do,' Eddie replied determinedly. 'But I need to find the keys to your cage. What's your name, little fella?' he asked.

'Monty,' the orangutan replied, 'and the keys are in that box on the wall.'

Flo looked on, amazed. It seemed that Eddie really could understand every animal on the planet, including orangutans. She suddenly felt very proud that he was her friend.

'I'll get the keys and then I'll get you out,' Eddie told Monty. 'Not a sound—'

But, before he could move, all the lights suddenly came on. Milo and OJ, the Bouncer Brothers hired by Vera, had been asleep on the job instead of watching the CCTV cameras.

Now, they'd suddenly woken up and were in the doorway, large and intimidating.

'Get them!' Milo shouted, rushing towards Eddie and Flo.

CHAPTER FORTY-ONE

Butch, who was a fearless little dog, rushed towards the brothers, barking angrily and baring his teeth.

As it happened, OJ was afraid of dogs, even little ones. He squealed and backed off but Milo, who wasn't scared of dogs at all, lashed out at Butch with his foot, sending him spinning across the shiny floor of the lab.

'Don't you kick my dog!' Eddie cried angrily, rushing at Milo with his fists clenched. 'I'm not scared of you.'

Milo, who was a lot bigger than Eddie, laughed scornfully. Grabbing the boy easily, he shoved him roughly under one arm. Eddie kicked and punched, struggling with all his might to get free, but the thug had a tight hold and there was no escape.

Spying a large spray can of disinfectant, Flo snatched it up and went on the attack. 'Put him down!' she demanded angrily, squirting the disinfectant at the thug.

Thinking it was something dangerous, Milo dropped Eddie immediately.

'Get her!' he shouted to OJ, who was shaking like a jelly with fear and standing on a chair in an attempt to escape from Butch, who was back on the defensive, yapping and snarling.

'Get him off me,' the thug whimpered. 'Pleeeeease!'

While this was going on, Monty was rattling the bars of his cage and screeching, the birds were making a racket, the mice and rats had started squeaking loudly, and even the rabbit was drumming his large back paws on the floor of his cage, making a loud thumping sound like a drum. The noise was deafening.

'Can someone kindly tell me just what is going on?' said a loud voice.

It was Vera, who'd been woken by the noise. She was a terrifying sight, standing there dressed in a black turban and lime-green nightie, her face slathered in cream. She was still attached to the drip that was connected to the bag containing the magic serum, hanging from a metal stand on wheels.

'Well, well, well,' she snarled, spotting Eddie and Flo. 'Lock 'em up in that empty cage,' she ordered Milo, 'and you – get down off that chair and deal with the dog.'

OJ grinned sheepishly, but he was shaking in his boots with fright and unable to move as Butch gave him the mean eye and growled menacingly at him.

Vera sighed in disbelief. 'Oh, you great steaming cowpat of a coward!' She marched determinedly towards Butch, grabbed him by the scruff of the neck and threw him into the empty cage. 'Now, see if you can manage to do the same to the brats. Lock them up. I've still got another few hours to go before my treatment is complete.'

The thugs were bigger and stronger than Flo and Eddie. Resistance was useless, and in no time the two children had joined Butch in the cage.

'What about our money?' one of the thugs asked, too scared to look Vera in the eye. 'You haven't paid us yet.'

'You'll get your cash,' Vera snapped back, 'even though you don't deserve it. Just get back in that office and keep a lookout for the cops.'

OJ and Milo slunk out, leaving Vera alone with the children.

'Thought you were being clever, didn't you?' she gloated,

peering at Eddie and Flo through the bars of the cage and setting Butch off growling. 'Well, look where it's got you. Now I've caught you, what plans do we have for you?' She smiled slyly to herself as if she'd just been struck by a diabolical idea. 'You're both young and healthy,' she said, eyeing them like the witch in Hansel and Gretel. 'And, as the good doctor is working on a new youth serum, I'm sure some of your fresh young plasma, not to mention those lovely little baby stem cells, might just provide a vital ingredient to give it that little boost. What do you think, eh, Flo?' she sneered, trying to goad the girl.

'My parents will find us,' Flo said angrily, certain that they would.

'So will Aunt Budge,' Eddie added. 'She's really smart. Smarter than you any day.'

Vera merely laughed. 'Oh, the optimism of youth,' she mocked, and then suddenly turning very angry, she thrust her greasy, cream-smeared face close to the cage. 'There's just one small detail that rules out you ever being rescued,' she hissed, dangling the keys to the cage on the end of her finger. 'Nobody knows you're here. More importantly, nobody ever will. Now, I'm going back to bed and I do not wish to be disturbed, but as soon as Dr Lockjaw emerges from his deep freezer in the basement, and my glorious treatment is complete, you two are going to become his guinea pigs. He wants to have a look at your brain, little boy, as he's extremely interested to discover how you can hold a conversation with that crow. Aren't you lucky?'

Cackling happily to herself, Vera almost skipped back towards her bedroom, the wheels of the drip stand squeaking as she dragged it alongside her. 'Get your rest now!' she shouted over her shoulder, returning the key to the box on the wall and turning off the lights before departing. 'Aunty Vera is going to need you nice and alert in the morning for all those lovely experiments.'

They sat in the dark for a moment, unsure what to do. Eventually, Flo asked in a worried voice, 'What now?'

'Somehow, we've got to get out of this cage,' Eddie replied, looking round at the heavy iron bars. 'But I don't see how. Have you got any ideas?'

Looking very miserable, Flo shook her head. '*Nay*,' she said in Dutch.

'Well, that's it, then,' Eddie said quietly. 'We've had it.'

CHAPTER FORTY-TWO

'Had it?' an outraged Bunty shouted, crawling out of Eddie's pocket and almost flying down his leg and on to the floor, huffing and puffing angrily.

'Had it?' she asked again, standing defiantly with her paws on her hips. 'Why, I've never heard such rot in all my born days. Do you think that my ancestors who landed on this soil all those centuries ago exclaimed, "Let's go home – we've had it,"? No! They stayed and turned marshland into a proud city and named it . . .' Here she paused and thumped her chest dramatically. 'We can't give up. I can slip through these bars and get the key out of that cabinet on the wall,' she said triumphantly.

'Can you really?' Eddie asked.

'Can she really what?' Flo asked, wondering what was going on.

'Get the key,' he explained as Bunty attempted to squeeze through the bars.

'Bit close together,' the hamster spluttered as she made another attempt to push herself through. The upper part of her body was halfway there. The problem was getting the rest of it to follow.

Monty, who was in the next cage to Eddie and Flo, had clearly never seen a hamster before. 'What is it?' he asked Eddie as he watched Bunty struggling to get through the bars. 'A fat mouse?'

'I heard that!' an indignant Bunty said, ceasing her endeavours for a moment and giving Monty a dirty look. 'I'm not a mouse, I'm a hamster.'

'Sorry,' Monty replied, lowering his head shyly; he hadn't meant to be rude.

'No offence taken,' Bunty told him, cheery again. 'You weren't to know. Now, all I need is to do a very lively wiggle and I might just slip through.'

'Shall I give her a little nip on the bum?' Butch offered. 'Maybe that would make her move herself.'

'You needn't bother, thank you very much,' Bunty gasped as she resumed her struggle. 'All it takes is the right –' and with one final heave she popped through the bars – 'manoeuvre,' she announced in between gasps as she got her breath back.

'Good work, Bunty!' said Eddie.

'Right. I'm going in to get those keys,' Bunty said, once she'd recovered. 'Wish me luck, chaps.' And saluting smartly she skittered off across the lab.

CHAPTER FORTY-THREE

The box that held the keys was high up on the wall. Also hanging on the wall, and conveniently placed near the cabinet, was a roller towel, and under that was a steel cabinet.

Having reached her destination, Bunty stood for a moment, contemplating the best and – more importantly – the easiest way to tackle the situation.

'If I climb the cabinet using those steel handles as a ladder . . . and then make my way up those containers on top of the cabinet . . . then I should be able to make it to the sink,' she said to herself. 'Then, if I jump high enough, I can reach that towel . . . crawl up it . . . and, by stretching out, I think I can just make it to the key box.'

When put like that, it sounded easy enough . . . kind of. However, even though she went for a long run every day on her wheel, Bunty wasn't quite as agile as she believed herself to be.

'Time to limber up, old gal,' she said, stretching herself to her full height and waggling her paws about. 'You've got a long ascent ahead of you.'

Climbing up the cabinet to the sink was fairly easy, but getting on to the roller towel was a lot more difficult. It took three attempts before she managed to leap high enough to grab hold of a corner. She hung there for a while to get her breath back before attempting to scale the roller.

She didn't find it at all difficult to climb the towel but, just as she'd made it to the middle, the laboratory lights suddenly came on.

It was Dr Lockjaw, accompanied by Miss Lubis.

Bunty swung herself round to make a fold in the towel and quickly hid inside it. 'Camouflage,' she murmured, remembering her training. 'The first rule of survival.' From among the folds of the fabric she listened intently to Lockjaw.

'Ah, our uninvited guests,' he was saying. 'Sneaky little thieves who think they can break into my laboratory and get away with it.'

'We came to rescue the orangutan you stole,' Eddie replied angrily. 'You're the thief, not us.'

Dr Lockjaw glared at him from behind his steel-rimmed

glasses. 'Wild accusations like that could get you into a lot of trouble,' he warned.

After instructing Miss Lubis to fetch the trolley and his equipment, he ordered OJ, who was sitting in the office with his brother, to get Eddie out of the cage. 'If he gives you any trouble, then don't be gentle with him,' Lockjaw instructed. 'Impudent children need to be disciplined.'

Of course, Eddie put up a fight, as did Flo, who bit OJ hard on the arm before receiving a blow across the head that made her dizzy. Butch wasn't having any of that and sank his teeth into OJ's leg, making him squeal and drop Eddie.

'Why the delay?' Dr Lockjaw demanded. 'Don't tell me you can't handle a ten-year-old? Just grab him.'

Eventually, after a bit more tussling, OJ managed to drag Eddie out by his hair. 'Where do you want him?' asked the thug, panting and rubbing the back of his leg where Butch had bitten him.

'Strap him down on the trolley, of course,' Lockjaw commanded. 'But first I want a little chat with our young friend before I begin the procedure.'

In the meantime, Butch was barking his head off and Flo was shouting all sorts of things in a mixture of Dutch, Portuguese and English. The little orangutan was screeching and banging on the bars of the cage and Eddie was making quite a racket too as OJ fought to strap him down on the trolley.

'Enough!' Lockjaw roared, instantly silencing everyone. 'Madame van Loon has almost completed her treatment and we wouldn't want to disturb her now, would we?' he warned as he leant over the trolley.

Flo felt totally helpless as she sat at the back of the cage. All she could do was watch whatever Lockjaw was going to do to Eddie.

'Don't worry,' Butch told her, jumping on to her lap. 'As soon as Bunty gets the keys to this cage, I'm going to have 'em.' It was just a shame Flo couldn't understand him.

'Now then, young man,' Lockjaw said casually, 'I've seen the CCTV footage of you and your friends, and it's most interesting, most interesting indeed. So tell me: how do you do it?'

'Do what?' Eddie asked angrily.

'Come, come, you know what I'm talking about. How did you learn to communicate with a crow? That was quite a conversation you two were having out there,' Lockjaw commented, removing his glasses and wiping them slowly with his handkerchief. 'Almost unbelievable, one might say. So how is it possible?'

'It's a trick, a magic trick,' Eddie started to explain, trying to sound convincing. 'I'm a ventriloquist. I can throw my voice.'

'Really?' said Lockjaw in mock surprise. 'Perhaps you'd like to give me a demonstration, then. Let's see if you can make it look as if Miss Lubis is saying something without moving your lips. Go on.'

Eddie gave it his best shot but it was a pretty awful attempt and Lockjaw wasn't fooled one bit.

'Just as I thought. You're no more a ventriloquist than I am,' he said, grim-faced. 'So let's stop fooling around, shall we? Why don't you just tell me how you managed to understand every croak that crow made?'

Eddie remained silent.

'Very well, have it your own way,' Dr Lockjaw said, holding a shiny instrument up to the light. 'The brain is a remarkable organ, so what I'm going to do is take a little peep at yours. All in the name of medical science, of course,' he said, smiling. 'I'm just going to whip the top of your head off. It's a bit like removing the shell from a hard-boiled egg only noisier and, I'm afraid, smellier.'

Eddie could see that Lockjaw was preparing various gleaming tools.

'Obviously, you'll have to be awake for this procedure because I'll need you to respond to my questions as I probe about in your brain. But don't worry; Miss Lubis will give you something to help numb the pain. After she's shaved your head, of course,' he said.

'Or . . . you could just send us home and we could all have an early night?' ventured Eddie.

'Don't be silly,' said Dr Lockjaw. 'Oh, and one more thing,' he added as he examined the saw, checking that it was sharp enough with the tip of his finger. 'There will be side effects from this operation, such as memory loss. You won't remember who your friends and family are, but I'm afraid that can't be helped. Now, shall we proceed?'

CHAPTER FORTY-FOUR

Eddie started to struggle furiously but the straps that held him down were tied tightly and there was no escape. Meanwhile, Miss Lubis was pleading with Lockjaw not to go ahead – and even OJ didn't seem very keen on the idea.

'I'm not getting involved in this. He's only a kid,' he grunted, but Lockjaw told him to mind his own business and do as he was told.

'Shave his hair off this minute,' Lockjaw ordered, grabbing Miss Lubis by the arm and shaking her hard. 'Then give him a mild anaesthetic, but not too much. I want him wide awake.'

Eddie closed his eyes tightly as he heard the buzz of the electric razor. But, as he lay there, he was sure he could hear another noise rising above the buzz. It was growing louder and louder. It sounded like . . . a helicopter!

Eddie opened his eyes and was instantly blinded by the bright search-beams shining through the skylight above him.

Suddenly, there was a loud smash as the glass broke and two figures appeared – one small, one tall and both dressed from head to toe in black – abseiling down from the roof into the lab. Miss Lubis dropped the razor and ran for cover.

'Get them!' Dr Lockjaw shouted to OJ and Milo, but before they had time to make a move the taller figure in black had thrown Milo over his shoulder, flipping him so he landed hard on the floor. Milo sat, stunned, but as he tried to get up off the floor the tall figure grabbed his ankle and arm and started swinging him round and round at such a speed that, when the tall figure let go, Milo went flying into an empty cage. Its door locked shut behind him.

Meanwhile, the shorter figure had adopted a karate pose. OJ stood laughing at the sight of this small person threatening him, but he wasn't grinning for very long. The small figure then delivered a lethal drop-kick right into a very tender part of his anatomy, causing OJ to fall to his knees.

What on earth? thought Eddie.

Then he spotted a large black crow flying in through the broken skylight, with a smaller bird on his back. 'Stanley!' Eddie shouted. 'Get the key off Bunty. She's over there in that box on the wall.'

'Will do,' Stanley cawed. 'Me and Casey to the rescue.'

Bunty had used the distraction to make her way up to the key box on the wall. She was now holding the key in one paw and hanging on to the door with the other, swinging back and forth.

'Catch!' she yelled, throwing the key to Stanley, who caught it in his beak. Flying over to the cage where Flo and Butch were imprisoned, the crow dropped it through the bars. Flo quickly unlocked the door and ran over to help the tall, mysterious figure undo the straps that held Eddie down on the trolley.

Groaning loudly, OJ had slowly risen to his feet. 'I'm going to tear you to tiny little pieces!' he roared, clenching his huge fists. 'Whoever you are.' But what he'd failed to notice was that Butch was now out of the cage and seeing a golden opportunity for revenge. The little dog leapt at OJ and bit him in that very same sensitive area where the rescuer in black had kicked him.

'Oooooooomph,' he wailed as he buckled.

Butch, though, had other ideas. 'It's time to play chase!' he barked, his tail wagging as he started to chase a squealing OJ round the lab, yapping and growling and having a fine old time.

During this commotion, Lockjaw had crept off and had been busy stuffing important-looking papers into his briefcase. Now, he had to escape and the only way was to make a run for it. Sneaking out of the room next to the one where Vera was sleeping, he ran straight into the little figure in black who'd been busy handcuffing OJ to the bars of his brother's cage.

'Dr Lockjaw, I presume,' the rescuer said, pulling off the balaclava. 'Just what do you think you're doing to my nephew and his friend?'

Eddie goggled in amazement at the face of the abseiling, drop-kicking figure. 'Aunt Budge!' he shouted happily, jumping down off the trolley.

CHAPTER FORTY-FIVE

'B ut how . . .? What . . .? Where . . .?' spluttered Eddie. He was totally confused, as was Flo, who couldn't really believe her eyes.

'It looks like we arrived just in time,' the taller figure said, pulling the balaclava off to reveal herself as Miss Schmidt. 'These things are hot,' she said, shoving the headwear into her pocket. Then she approached Dr Lockjaw.

Seizing his chance, the doctor grabbed a syringe off a trolley and jabbed it into Miss Schmidt's arm. It contained a sedative and within seconds she'd slumped to the floor, fast asleep. Snatching up a lethal-looking buzz saw, much bigger than the one he'd been about to use on Eddie, Lockjaw threw his arm round Aunt Budge's neck and started to back towards the door, holding her tightly.

'Don't any of you move,' he snarled as he kept reversing, 'or she gets it.'

Eddie muttered something under his breath but Lockjaw warned him off. That buzz saw was deadly and he was holding it dangerously close to Aunt Budge's face.

Meanwhile, Stanley and Casey were perched on top of the box, watching.

'I'm going to dive-bomb him,' Stanley whispered to Casey. 'Wish me luck.' And he took off, aiming straight for Lockjaw's head. Unfortunately for Stanley, though, Lockjaw was too quick for him, and he lashed out with the buzz saw, catching the crow's wing and sending him crashing into the wall. The brave Liver Bird fell in a heap on the floor and lay there, silent and motionless.

'Stanley!' Eddie cried.

'Leave it,' Lockjaw ordered. 'Let it die.'

From the top of the box Casey let out a mournful screech. Flapping his wings angrily, he told himself that if ever there was a time he needed to summon up the energy and confidence to fly then this was it. The man had killed his friend and he had to be stopped.

Bracing himself, the parrot took off, a little unsteadily to start with. At first he looked as if he was going to crash-land on the floor, but with a burst of energy he built up momentum and soared upwards, swooping on Lockjaw and knocking his glasses off.

Lockjaw lashed out with the buzz saw but missed Casey, who swooped again, pecking the doctor's hand so hard that he dropped the weapon.

Lockjaw threw Aunt Budge out of the way and made a dash for the door, but Eddie and Butch were after him. Eddie brought him down with a magnificent rugby tackle that would've shut his PE teacher up (because he'd never thought Eddie was any good at rugby).

Then Flo joined in the chase, getting a little ahead of Lockjaw, who was struggling to get up as Eddie and Butch clung on to him. The doctor was almost up on his knees, even though Eddie was now hanging off his neck and Butch had his teeth firmly clenched on Lockjaw's bottom.

'Going somewhere?' Flo asked, delivering a perfect uppercut and knocking the doctor out cold.

Eddie stared at her, wide-eyed, as he slid off Lockjaw's back.

'I told you, I go to boxing classes – remember?' Flo said to Eddie, blowing on her knuckles. 'He deserved that.'

But Eddie didn't hear because he'd rushed over to where Stanley was crumpled on the floor. The crow lay in a strange position, his wing bent unnaturally underneath him.

'Stan,' Eddie coaxed, kneeling down beside the bird and gently placing a hand on his feathers, 'wake up! Don't go, mate; stay with me . . . please.'

But Stanley lay silent, his eyes closed. Eddie bowed his

head as he stroked his old friend and felt the hot tears running down his face. 'This is all my fault,' he sobbed. 'If we hadn't come here, this wouldn't have happened.'

Aunt Budge knelt down beside Eddie, putting her arm round him. 'Don't blame yourself, my dear. Of course this isn't your fault,' she said softly. 'Stanley was such a remarkable bird, so full of life. It's a terrible tragedy and that man will pay for it.'

Butch lay beside Stanley, gently nudging him with his nose in an attempt to rouse him. 'Come on, you, get up,' he was saying. 'Who am I going to fight with if you're not around?'

'It's no good, Butch,' Eddie said gently. 'He's gone.'

Flo stood silently, unable to hold back the tears, with a very subdued Casey sitting on her shoulder. Even Miss Schmidt, who'd woken just in time to tie Dr Lockjaw up, was blowing her nose.

Then . . .

'Hang about, I ain't going anywhere,' a familiar voice croaked.

CHAPTER FORTY-SIX

I t was Stanley, and he was very much alive!

'I think I've done my wing in,' he croaked, 'and I've got a bit of an 'eadache, but apart from that I'll live. Now then, folks,' he said with a devilish twinkle in his eye, 'has anything exciting happened while I was having a kip?'

They all cheered and clapped loudly. Eddie wiped his eyes, picked Stanley up very carefully and held him in his arms. 'Don't worry,' he said. 'I'll soon have you fixed up.' And, giving him a little squeeze, he said, 'I love you, Stanley.'

'I love you too, kid,' Stanley replied, 'but mind my wing.'

'You're a hero!' Casey screeched. 'You deserve a medal.'

'So do you,' Aunt Budge told him. 'The way you flew across the lab and disarmed that awful man.'

So they all cheered again.

'Talking of heroes,' Eddie said suddenly, 'where's Bunty?'

After making her spectacular leap on to the catch of the key box, Bunty had found that the door hadn't been closed properly so it now swung open with Bunty hanging on to it for dear life. Even though she'd managed to get the key to Stanley and her mission had been successful, she was getting tired of swinging about and wondered when somebody would come and rescue her.

At that moment, it just so happened that Vera, having awoken from her stupor but still a little groggy from the medicine, came staggering out of her room for the second time, demanding to know what all the noise was about. As she lurched past the key box, the door swung straight towards her face and Bunty took the opportunity to let go, crashing into Vera's cheek and clinging on to the lady's whiskers . . .

Whiskers? Vera had whiskers?

Vera screamed. Bunty screamed too, letting go and falling to the floor, then scurrying off towards Eddie and the others.

'There was a rat on my face!' Vera shrieked, slapping her cheek and feeling around to make sure the creature had gone. 'It's still there!' She screamed louder than ever, grabbing what she believed to be a tail and pulling it hard.

'Ow!' she bellowed as it slowly dawned on her that it wasn't a rat's tail at all. It was her moustache. The doctor's serum had most definitely worked, but now she not only had hair on her head, she was also covered in it all over. Shaggy, bright orange hair. In fact, she was now hairier than the baby orangutan, who was out of his cage and happily holding Eddie's hand.

They all stared, open-mouthed in disbelief, at the extremely hairy Vera, who now resembled a ginger yeti.

Eventually, Aunt Budge spoke. 'Vera, my dear,' she said, 'did you forget to shave this morning?'

After taking a good look at herself in the mirror above the sink to see what Aunt Budge had meant, Vera fell into a dead faint.

CHAPTER FORTY-SEVEN

'How did you know we were here?' Eddie asked Aunt Budge as Whetstone arrived with the police.

'Stanley, that unbelievably intelligent crow, told me. I didn't want to waste any time and as the gyrocopter was handily parked on the roof we simply jumped in and followed him here.'

'Did you just say you had a gyrocopter on the roof?' Eddie asked in amazement, unable to believe his ears.

'Yes, dear,' Aunt Budge replied nonchalantly, as if it were the most normal thing in the world. 'Didn't you notice? There's a cover over it.'

'I thought that was just a barbecue you'd covered up.'

'Yes, well, the copter is only a little one,' she said, 'but I doubt if you could grill a sausage on it.'

'But you abseiled in,' Eddie said, astounded. 'Like in a spy film. Wow!'

'Yes, dear,' Aunt Budge said matter-of-factly. 'I've been abseiling for years. I've lots of hobbies – the martial arts are another one of mine. Miss Schmidt is a black belt in both judo and karate, you know. She's also an admirable kick-boxer,' she added with a hint of pride in her voice.

'Wow,' Flo said in awe. 'These old ones certainly know how to kick butt.'

'Less of the old,' Miss Schmidt retorted. 'Don't forget you're talking to a lady who once wrestled an alligator.'

Meanwhile, the police didn't know whether to take Vera to a vet or the police station as they couldn't quite make out what she was.

'She's Mrs Veronica van Loon,' Aunt Budge explained to a perplexed policeman. 'A so-called human being. One you'll find is responsible for a multitude of crimes, including the kidnapping of two children and an orangutan.'

The police officer didn't really know what to say to that, but he duly arrested Vera, whose muffled shouts could be heard coming from beneath a mountain of hair. 'I want my lawyer . . . and a hairdresser!'

'Well, good riddance to bad rubbish!' Aunt Budge exclaimed as she watched the mane of ginger hair that was

Vera being carried out of the door. 'Now, it'll soon be sunrise so it's about time we all went home and had an early breakfast. That . . . or a very late supper, depending on how you look at it. Come along, you two. Miss Schmidt can go back in the car with Whetstone and the animals, and you two can come with me in the gyrocopter.'

Flo and Eddie looked at each other. 'Do you remember when I said nothing exciting ever happens and every day is the same?' she asked him.

'Yes, why?' Eddie asked.

'Well, I take it all back,' Flo replied. 'Every single word.'

Aunt Budge had climbed the metal ladder on to the roof of the lab and flown the gyrocopter down on to the grass outside. 'Hop in!' she shouted above the noise of the whirling blades. 'And don't forget to duck. Or, indeed, that I shall want a very strong word with both of you when we get back,' she added. 'Now, put your helmets on and fasten your seat belts. There will be a lovely view of Amsterdam from up here.'

CHAPTER FORTY-EIGHT

T he ride home was exhilarating but once they'd landed on the roof and were sitting in Aunt Budge's morning room she gave them both a real dressing-down.

'It was a foolish, reckless thing to do,' she scolded. 'You could both have been killed if we hadn't arrived in the nick of time.'

Flo's parents weren't exactly thrilled with their daughter, either, and Eddie's dad had quite a lot to say as well when they spoke on FaceTime.

'Dad!' Eddie shouted, after they connected on Aunt Budge's computer. 'Dad, I've missed you but wait until I tell you this—'

Eddie's dad interrupted him. 'I know all about your escapades,' he said, not sounding in the least bit happy. 'And I want to know what on earth you were thinking, putting yourself in such danger, getting involved with mad scientists and evil women, just to rescue an animal? Think of your aunt. She was worried sick!'

Eddie tried to explain but Dad cut him off again.

'Eddie?'

'Yes, Dad?'

'I'm surprised at you taking such risks . . . but . . . I have to admit . . . that I'm also very proud.' Then Dad started to laugh.

Eddie breathed a sigh of relief. 'I thought you were angry with me,' he said.

'Not angry exactly, just very worried,' his dad replied. 'I couldn't quite believe what I was reading online, but then I always knew I had a brave, gutsy, thoroughly decent young man for a son.' Was that a tear in Dad's eye or simply a trick of the light? Eddie wasn't quite sure. 'Right then,' his dad continued cheerily, after blowing his nose, 'I've had some news as well. I received a letter from the director of the Royal Philharmonic Orchestra. They're looking for a solo guitarist! I don't know how they knew about me, but they've offered me the job – and I wouldn't have to travel; I could stay at home. For the first time since your mum died I got my guitar out and played . . . and it felt good.'

'Are you going to take the job?' Eddie asked eagerly, pleased that his dad seemed to be getting back to his old self.

His dad laughed. 'I know one thing – I'm not cut out to be the manager of a supermarket. I'm not smart enough. It's a tough job, believe me, so I think it's best if I go back to music.'

Aunt Budge, who had stayed in the room during their conversation, was also quietly delighted that Eddie's dad was taking the job. He would never find out, but she was the one who'd got in touch with her old friend the orchestra director and put Dad's name forward for the vacancy.

'See you in a week or so,' Dad said, 'and no more adventures!'

Eddie chuckled to himself. In his wildest dreams, he wouldn't have believed what a remarkable escapade he'd just been a part of. The holiday had flown by and so much had happened during that time. Eddie had made a good friend of his own age, someone he could be himself with. Plus, he'd done and seen some amazing things. He'd also found himself in the kind of danger that he'd thought only happened in films and in the pages of his superhero comics.

It wasn't long before Eddie, Flo and Aunt Budge became the talk of the internet, and they were very soon plastered all over the newspapers. Journalists and paparazzi gathered outside Aunt Budge's house, much to her annoyance, until eventually, to make them go away, she agreed to pose on the front steps along with Eddie, Flo, Miss Schmidt, Whetstone and the animals. Even Stanley made sure he got in on this photo opportunity, sitting on the top step with his wing in a sling and smiling proudly.

Casey, having discovered the use of his wings again, sat on the big lantern that hung over the front door, whistling his head off to make sure that the photographers caught his best side.

Aunt Budge had pulled out all the stops for this photo session and was resplendent in a lilac flowery dress with a large hat trimmed with artificial flowers to match. Eddie was wearing his new jacket and looked very smart, even if Bunty was sitting on his head, grinning. Flo looked very chic in a black sweater and trousers, holding Butch, who was wearing his poncho to make sure everyone knew he was a real Mexican bandit. (Even though he'd grown to like his new tartan coat, he'd insisted that Eddie brought his poncho as well.)

The fish were also very keen to be in the photo, even though they'd had no part in the drama. So Eddie put them in their travelling tank, which he proudly held up for the flashing cameras, as the photographers shouted out instructions to turn this way and that, and face this camera on the end, please.

'Just listen to this,' Aunt Budge said the next day, wrinkling her nose in disgust as she read aloud from a newspaper. '"Lady

Buddleia, who is related to Her Majesty Queen Elizabeth . . ."
Who writes this rubbish?' she exclaimed, tapping her foot
angrily on the floor. 'I've only ever said hello to her once or
twice, never mind being related to the dear woman. I'll send
a letter of apology to the palace immediately, explaining that
I had nothing to do with such lies. I shall also demand an
apology from this dreadful newspaper.'

Eddie and Flo laughed, as they quite liked it when Aunt
Budge lost her temper.

They'd been shy about all the fuss at first, particularly
Eddie, who hated drawing attention to himself. The mayor
of Amsterdam had presented them with a medal each, and
even Queen Maxima had sent her congratulations on their
bravery. But, despite all of that, the best news was still Dad's
new job.

As for the animals in Lockjaw's lab, they were sent off to
good homes and Eddie was photographed handing Monty, the
young orangutan, back to his mother at the zoo. She'd gently
taken her baby from Eddie and cuddled him, staring at the boy
for a moment with big soulful eyes.

'Thank you,' she said. 'Thank you . . . friend.'

*

Eddie loved Amsterdam, especially lying in bed listening to the bells of the *Westerkerk* chime every quarter of an hour. He loved the houses that lined the canals, in particular Aunt Budge's with its endless stairs leading to large, spacious rooms with ornate mirrors and sparkling chandeliers.

He was going to miss lots of things – Aunt Budge, kind and unpredictable, and unlike anyone he'd ever met before. The boat trips with Flo. Sitting in the basement kitchen with Whetstone and Miss Schmidt, watching people's legs go past the window. The wheels of carriages carrying tourists, and the horses' hooves making that distinctive clip-clop noise as they went past. Sometimes, as he sat at the old kitchen table, eating a delicious pastry and watching the activity outside the window, he felt as if he'd gone back in time. Yes, he was certainly going to miss Amsterdam.

Flo had given him a kiss and a hug when they said goodbye, causing Eddie to turn beetroot-red. 'Friends for life?' she asked him.

'Friends for life,' Eddie replied, and they linked little fingers to seal their promise.

In fact, Flo was also going to England to visit Eddie next Easter, as after Aunt Budge had finished travelling she planned to open up her house on the Romney Marshes in Kent. She had invited both Eddie and Flo to stay for the holidays.

'You arrived here a shy, rather withdrawn little boy, and now look at you,' a tearful Aunt Budge declared proudly as they said goodbye. 'You've blossomed into a confident young man and shown that you possess a true sense of decency and a brave heart,' she gushed dramatically, dabbing the corner of her eyes with her handkerchief. 'I shall miss you and your beautiful animals terribly. You've been blessed with a unique

and extraordinary gift, Eddie; don't be ashamed of it. On the contrary, be proud of your talents as I think you'll find they will enhance your existence. Life can be a big adventure, my dear. All you need to do is allow it to happen. Now, off you go,' she said, sniffing and giving him an enormous kiss. 'Whetstone is waiting downstairs to drive you home.'

As he was about to get into the car, Aunt Budge shouted from the front step. 'One last thing. We old people don't all sit on the sofa watching daytime quiz shows, you know!' She gave him a wink. 'We have a wealth of experience and knowledge, plus a real zest for living, so never underestimate a more mature citizen because you may be surprised to find out what they're really like. Promise?'

'I promise,' Eddie replied, laughing.

As they drove through Holland, Eddie began to feel sleepy. Butch was already snoozing on his knee, while Bunty had curled up in his jacket pocket and could be heard snoring. The fish were nowhere to be seen as they'd retired behind the rocks in their travelling tank, annoyed that they were on the move again.

Eddie's eyes felt heavy and he could sense that he was

drifting off as they drove down the motorway. What was it Aunt Budge had said? Life is an adventure?

Well, she certainly got that right, he thought dreamily. And with that he fell asleep.

EPILOGUE

In case you're wondering what happened to the others, which you probably are . . . well, Dr Lockjaw is in jail awaiting trial and, according to the press, will probably stay there for the rest of his life. The two Bouncer Brothers were given the choice of going to jail or doing community service. As they didn't like the sound of jail, they opened a martial-arts school for children, which I've heard is a huge success. Miss Lubis had her passport returned, plus the money Vera owed her, and was finally able to go home to her family in Indonesia.

As for Vera, well, she was placed in a secure institution for the criminally insane, where she remains to this day, still covered in the bright orange hair she always wanted, even though they have to shave her every morning.

Casey charmed the pants off Flo's parents and they agreed to adopt him. Now, he sits on a perch in the window of their front room in Amsterdam, adored by Flo, swearing like a trooper and singing to his heart's content.

Stanley stayed with Aunt Budge until his wing healed and, when he was strong enough, flew back to England. Maggie, on whom he'd had a bit of a crush at first, had moved in with another magpie, which suited Stanley just fine as he'd gone off her by then. Besides, he told himself, he wasn't ready to enter into a long-term relationship just yet. Especially with the likes of Maggie.

Oh, and by the way, there's one more thing. Aunt Budge had given Eddie an envelope to pass on to his dad. Inside were the deeds to a nice little house not far from their current flat. There was also a letter from Aunt Budge.

Now I'm reunited with you both, I'm going to need somewhere to stay when I visit, so I'd be most grateful if you'd accept this gift and leave the spare room free for me.

Oh, and just one more thing – Eddie got his phone.